THE ROUTE

The Forgotten Side of Vieques

Pragmacio

ATHENA PRESS
LONDON

THE ROUTE: *The Forgotten Side of Vieques*

ISBN 1 931456 24 0

First Published 2004 by
ATHENA PRESS
Queen's House, 2 Holly Road
Twickenham TW1 4EG
United Kingdom

Printed for Athena Press

THE ROUTE

The Forgotten Side of Vieques

Dedication

For William Jefferson Clinton, former president of the United States, and Pedro Rossello, former governor of Puerto Rico, for their efforts to preserve for this planet a jewel in the Caribbean; for Ruben Berrios for his one year's self-confinement, being loyal to his principles and beliefs; for the remaining people of Vieques and for all the hundreds of thousands of U.S. navy and U.S. Marine Corps personnel who have visited and used this island for the last six decades, either to work on or to train themselves to protect our nation and preserve our system forever for the betterment of mankind. I also dedicate these memories to my sons and daughters who were anxious to read about the ancient lifestyle at the beginning of my life

I also want to thank Mr. Ramon Luis Ortiz, president of Ortiz Metal Works in Naranjito P.R., for his contribution on making the publication of this book possible.

This project was supported by the National Endowment for the Arts through the support to the Arts Office of the Institute of Puerto Rican Culture.

Finally, I dedicate this book to all the readers who take some time for reading and entertainment.

Preface

These stories about the island of Vieques took place sometime between the thirties and the fifties.

The book has been divided into fifty-seven stories. Although they are written in chronological order, they do not follow a sequential relation with one another. These are real stories about real places with real people, who lived during those days and of course passed away years ago. But still, some people in Vieques remember them.

The western portion of the island was returned by the U.S. navy to the municipality of Vieques. Now it is possible to walk through on the route starting at the site of Playa Grande.

A table of contents is included on the following pages for the reader to select and read any story without following a specific order or sequence.

Contents

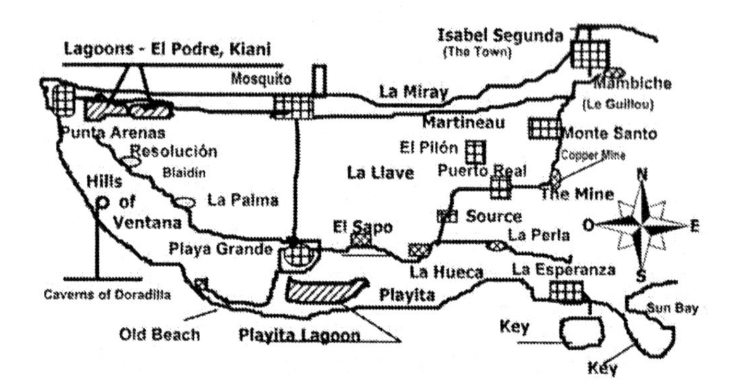

Vieques West (Circa 1938)

Introduction

Before the occupation by Europeans, the island of Vieques was inhabited by indigenous people named Caribs and Arawaks. After the colonization of Puerto Rico by Juan Ponce de Leon, Spain safeguarded this island from other Europeans who wanted to settle there.

At the beginning of the nineteenth century, a Frenchman named Theodore Le Guillou asked permission from Spain to colonize the island. He founded the sugar industry on this island with a large group of French farmers, engineers and technical personnel whose descendants still live on the island. He became the first governor of Vieques, founded the first city named Isabel Segunda and the first sugar mill named Santa Maria. Sugar was the main industry and there were four sugar mills, eight locomotives and three seaports until 1940 when the occupation by the U.S. navy made it disappear together with most of its population.

These stories describe the people that I knew during the course of my life, the places where they lived, their customs, and some of the serious and funny incidents that occurred during their life.

Playa Grande and El Sapo (The Beginning)

It was on a cool early morning that my mother came to the room in a hurry. She removed the mosquito net from the top of my hammock, woke me up and put me down. Quickly, I ran to the window looking to the east. There I observed the first sunlight on that beautiful morning. There were not too many clouds and the few that were there in the sky were bathed with the morning colors of red, yellow and silver. The sounds of pots and pans, the moos of the cattle, the bleat of the goats, the melodious morning songs of the roosters, the cackle of the hens, the peeps of the chickens, the smell of burnt wood from the kitchens, the rushing men and women getting ready for work, came together as a cacophony for the senses. I went outdoors where I could see women rushing around in their kitchens, cooking breakfast and lunch for their husbands to take to work. Men milking cows and goats and others moving cattle to the nearby pastures. Others with hoes on their shoulders or machetes under their arms, ready to start working on their farms, on their gardens or on a distant farm. It was the time of zafra, the sugarcane harvesting period. I could also hear the squeaks of the oxen-driven wagons' wheels while moving out to the cut cane fields.

My mother approached me and said, "Get ready, we have to go down to Playa Grande to your father's barber shop. You need a haircut. Put on your khaki trousers and the blue shirt, but hurry up because I want you to be the first."

"I am hungry, Mom," I said.

"Okay, come over to the kitchen, I'll give you a cup of coffee and a piece of arepa."

I ate my arepa, drank my coffee and got dressed rapidly. It was very pleasant, and like other children, I loved walking out with mother. My mother grabbed my little hand, and started walking down the hill until we reached the main road westwards to Playa Grande.

At this point we started the route to our destiny. Where was destiny taking us? Where to? How? Why? And for what purpose? The years to come in the future would be the witness of those events that were taking us through an arduous and difficult way through life.

We continued walking west over that dusty and narrow road. Looking towards the west, I could see two tall smoking chimneys. Farther west, I could see the hills of Ventana bathed by the light of the morning sun, and all the houses of the people who lived on the slopes of the hills. Down to the south of the road, I could see the locomotive roaring up the railway tracks moving towards La Hueca to get loaded with the sugarcane bales to be transported to La Central. Farther south, the mangroves circled the lagoon. The sound of the waves of the Caribbean sea and the waving movements of the coconut palm trees caused by the wind made me imagine that they were dancing and celebrating that splendid morning.

Up to the north, there were the recently cut sugarcane fields that produced a delicious aroma mixed with the cool and moisturized air of the morning. I could see men loading trucks with canes and the oxen-driven wagons moving towards the steep hills or glens where the trucks could not reach. We walked across the wooden bridge over El Chino's brook. The fierce currents of the brook caused the deaths of many people who tried to cross it during the rainy season.

I recall that at that time I was about four years old. My father had his barber shop on the north side of the road, in front of La Central. On the west side of the barber shop he also had a woodworking shop. The woodworking shop was a rustic construction made with cut wood from trees, roofed with old and rusty metal sheets. It was an open place with no walls. When we reached the place, my father was trying to repair the cabin of a station wagon. During those days the cabins of station wagons were partially built with wood. So, it was a woodworker's job to repair them when damaged.

My mother left me in front of the barber and woodworking shop. She did not talk to my father, not even a single word, and said to me, "When your haircut is over, just stay out here until I call for you."

"Yes, Mom," I said.

Before leaving, my mother kissed me on the cheek and with a mother's smile walked west down the street. I saw her crossing the street towards the south and then disappear from sight behind the other houses. At that moment I decided to get into the barber shop. There was a smell of talc and perfumes that mixed with the odors of molasses and burnt grease of La Central. The used talc spread all over on the floor was mixed with locks of cut hair. There were some pieces of paper also spread out on the floor. It seemed that my father had had little time to clean up the shop the night before. There were two barber's seats and near the wall he had two cabinets with one mirror each. On top of those cabinets he kept all the barber's tools and the cosmetics used for his work.

My father stopped working on the wagon, came in, lifted and seated me on a board that he put on top of the handles of the barber seat. He did a quick job. He did not talk to me, just put me down and walked to his woodworking shop. Then I walked out and observed the activities in and around La Central.

To the east, there was a photographer's shop belonging to a man named Alicea who had crippled feet. He was born with his feet bent or twisted towards the inside of his body. He wore special shoes made locally by a shoemaker.

South across the street, there was a big wall named La Plaza. It was round-shaped, made with rocks, bricks and concrete. The top of that huge wall was used to pile up the bales of cut cane prior to processing. There were two cranes on top of La Plaza. The crane closer to the street was used to unload the bales from trucks, from the oxen-driven wagons and from the locomotive wagons. The crane farther south from the street was used for feeding the mouth of La Central. They moved the bales, tied up with a special chain that had a lock that unlocked itself with a certain movement of the crane. The bales of sugarcane got loose and fell into the hole. The chains stood hanging on the hooks of the crane and were removed manually. There were eight locomotives serving La Central. The railways were located towards the west to Blaidin and Punta Arenas, north to Mosquito and Martineau, and east to La Hueca. On all those points there were winches operated by mules in order to load the trucks and locomotive wagons. On these winches, the oxen-driven wagons transferred their loads to trucks or to the locomotive wagons to speed up the transportation. Since the oxen were so slow they slowed down the traffic on the narrow roads. Locomotives were used to move loads of molasses, sugar and other products to Punta Arenas' seaport pier to be shipped out to other countries overseas. They were also used to move commercial merchandise and fuel moving in and out through this seaport.

Looking to the west, I could see a trough in the middle of the street facing north west. Across the street to the north, there was the office of La Central and close to it the dispensary. Right by the office, there was a man sitting on a home-made wooden cart. His name was Guarepa. He was a crippled short man who had his big toes separated from front to heel. He could not stand up straight. He tied up his toes with rubber bands that he found on the streets. He made this cart with a little seat, over four wheels taken from old tricycles. He sat in front of the office to ask for charity money in order to support himself. He was all hairy with a big black mustache. His face was all twisted and looked more like a chimpanzee than a human. Nobody knew his origin. He talked very little, using a strange language or dialect. As mysteriously as he appeared in Vieques, so was his disappearance. Nobody could tell where he went to, if he died on some unknown site or just got off the island.

The street going north was named The Millions, perhaps because the people who lived there were of good economic means. Walking north on The Millions street and to the right side, the machine shop was located. Toolmakers, machinists and other mechanic workers served La Central and the community from this shop. Towards the southwest and across the tracks, there were the two stores belonging to Don Manolo and to Don Oscar. Don Manolo sold garments and fabrics. Don Oscar's store was dedicated to groceries. He had an employee named Juan who, after the expropriation, started his own grocery store at Monte Santo. He became a very prosperous businessman until his retirement.

La Central had a very powerful power generator that, like the locomotives, was operated with coal. That generator served the town of Playa Grande, Mosquito, Blaidin and Punta Arenas. The posts, which carried the power lines to all those towns, were located alongside the rail tracks. There was some illumination at night on the few streets in Playa Grande. They had poles with porcelain fixtures that were green on the top and beige at the bottom, where the incandescent lamp was installed. On the nights that I spent in that place I observed that the lights were very dim.

In the sugar mills during those days, there were four types of housing. There was housing for the technical personnel like electricians, drivers, machine operators, locomotive engineers, plumbers and others. There was housing for the white collar workers and professionals, housing for the poorest of workers with no dexterity, and the pranganas that were the quarters for the migrant workers who came from Puerto Rico and other Caribbean islands. These pranganas were of a very poor appearance. They were long buildings with no rooms. Some of the workers used to put old sacks or pieces of cloth to make a separate room on their own. They were of such a bad look that when people were in a bad economic condition they used to say, "I am in the prangana."

Down to the west of La Central and towards the south, there was a street named the street of Fire. It was a dirty street, covered with soot. All the houses were covered with the soot that was produced at La Central, coming out through the chimneys into the atmosphere. I noticed that the faces of almost all the people who lived there were covered with that black soot. The poorest people in this neighborhood lived on this dirty street in shabby houses. It was named the Fire Street because of the many crimes and suicides that happened by using these means. Many young girls and boys committed suicide using this way, simply because they were forsaken by their loved ones.

Some used to pour gasoline over his or her body, light a match and form human torches until the fire consumed them. I was told that most of the time it happened close to midnight.

One of the most notorious cases was the one told by the son of Maria. He was a disabled veteran from the Second World War and the Korean conflict. He was wounded several times by the enemy's fire until he was disabled. Now immersed in alcoholism, he always repeats the same story. He says that when he was five years old, his mother got very jealous of his father and that one night she waited for him with a pot of boiling water. As soon as he entered the house that night she poured that pot of boiling water on his father and killed him.

After a long wait, I saw my mother coming from the west and ran into her arms. She lifted me, gave me a kiss and put me down.

"Mom, how big is La Central?"

"Yes, son, it is very big"

"Can we get in, Mom?"

"No, we cannot get in, because it is too dangerous for kids to get close to all those big machines. Only people who work in there are allowed to walk in."

"Some day in the future, I will be able to walk inside La Central, Mom."

"Yes, dear, in the future you may be able to work there."

With my mind full of kids' illusions, my mother took my hand and started to walk towards the street of Fire. We stopped and entered the house of one of Mother's friend. When they started to talk the way women do, I got out of the house to observe the surroundings. I noticed that the windows and doors of the house had old sacks hanging outside to prevent or minimize the effects of the soot coming down from the chimneys. I also noticed that the soot came down in a gusty way, depending on which way the wind blew. The street was all dusty black. Down the street, I saw a hill named the Goat's Hill. On the south side of this hill, there was a quarry from where all the rocks used for roads and rail tracks were taken from.

I remember the way they used to build the roads. The workers cleaned the way with hoes and picks. Then, a large group of workers put the rocks manually side by side on the way. After all the rocks were in place they used a twenty-ton roller to flatten them. After flattening these rocks, they put molten tar, and covered them up with shovels of sand. All this was done manually, except for the roller and the wheelbarrows used to transport the rocks and the sand. The rail tracks were also built and maintained manually. The tar used to pave the roads came in fifty-five gallon drums transported in vessels from the state of Texas down to the seaport of Punta Arenas.

After my mother's conversation was over, we walked back home. She stopped for a while at Don Oscar's store. From the sidewalk of Don Oscar's store, to the north, I saw the stables of Cunda, the blacksmith, and to the west, the rail tracks on their way to Blaidin. There was a road to the south named La Toma. On this road, not too far down, was located the fresh water well that served La Central and the rest of the neighborhood. It was very deep and its pump was about nine feet to the west from it. I could not observe more because my mother quickly got out of the store and we continued our way east to our home.

Down to the south of the road, not too far, there was the fresh water lagoon named Playita Lagoon. The two brooks that fed the lagoon were El Sapo and El Chino. The brook El Sapo was located to the east of the community of the same name where my mother lived with my other brothers, sisters and myself. On our way back home through that dusty road, we had to move quickly to the side of it every time a truck came by. It was a very uncomfortable walk. By the time we reached home, I was all tired and hungry. My feet hurt and I felt fatigued with the heat of that day. Quickly, I laid down on the floor, right by the front door, to relax. It was close to noon when we reached home and I was hungry. My mother came to me and said, "Come to the kitchen to get a piece of cake with a glass of milk. I have to take care of the baby."

My younger sister was only a few months old and my other brothers and sister were attending school in Puerto Real. Aunt Juanita took care of the baby girl while we were in Playa Grande. We lived in aunt Juanita's house. We occupied two rooms of the house until we could find a place to live in. At that time my mother and father were separated and they did not talk to each other. My mother had to do some domestic work like laundering, cooking and she also did some light farming works like harvesting garden vegetables in order to support us.

Farming activities were hectic during the zafra period. Cutting the canes with machetes, cleaning up the plantations with hoes after the cut, replacing old plantations with new seeds and the fertilizing of terrain was done with extreme dedication. The farming of garden vegetables, the bananas and corn plantations, together with the sugarcane, extended throughout the entire island. Around the houses, they used to plant the herbs and spices used for cooking. Every cooked dish was made with freshly harvested ingredients. There was no method of preserving food during those days, except for the salted seafood or pork meats. There were also medicinal plants around the houses.

Animals like goats, cows, chickens and guinea fowls were kept close to the homes, except for the larger cattle farms used for dairies. Some others had larger farms to grow on a large scale white sweet potatoes, corn, tomatoes, tobacco, cotton and other indigenous roots used as food. These farms were very important during the times of Bruja. Bruja was the time when the zafra period came to an end, the unemployment rate was high and money was difficult to get.

The dairies around used stainless steel containers of three sizes to distribute the fresh milk. They used one liter, one gallon and the big one of about five gallons. The man who came to our neighborhood in the early mornings used a cart built with wood and covered with metal sheets. The cart rolled on two big wooden wheels pushed by a long wooden pole. Inside that cart he also carried freshly baked bread, crackers and cookies to sell for breakfast.

There was another person who visited our neighborhood. That person was named the Investigator. He had a four-wheel cart in which he carried all kinds of hand tools. He was the "repairman" for everything. He had grinding wheels to sharpen all kinds of tools, including scissors, tools to straighten bed springs, repair sewing machines and many others. He was a smart man whom everybody was afraid of because of his tricky way of doing business.

My mother told me that years before there were four sugar mills on the island. There was one in Blaidin, one in La Esperanza and one in Santa María. Santa María, east of Isabel Segunda, was the first sugar mill on the island founded by Theodore Le Guillou. There was another small sugar processor in Source whose owner was Don Antonio. He made Mascabado sugar. That kind of sugar was made in bars, not granulated. Some people liked this type of sugar to sweeten the black coffee rather than the white sugar because of its special taste.

Pocito, Playa Vieja

Southeast of Playa Grande, and across the last of the hills of Ventana, there were two small villages named Pocito (Little Well), and Playa Vieja (Old Beach). These were located very close to the beach and circled by a forest of coconut palm trees. For me, that area was one of the most beautiful places ever on this planet. The forest of palm trees was located on a tiny peninsula where the beach was so shallow that anyone could walk into the sea, hundreds of feet in. There were corals of many colors, like a colorful landscape. Thousands of colorful tiny fishes played, getting in and out of the corals and other seaweeds in the area. The water was crystal clear with no polluted elements. Everything was clean and clear. I enjoyed watching that spectacular show of nature by chasing the tiny fish without harming them. In the forest of palm trees there was one that used to bear a big coconut that had about one gallon of water inside it. That one was my favorite because only one coconut was enough to peel and drink its delicious water. In those villages lived the Romero and the Ortiz families. After the expropriation the Romero family moved to the Le Guillou neighborhood and the Ortiz family moved to La Hueca.

Punta Arenas, La Palma, Resolucion

Northwest of Playa Grande was located the seaport of Punta Arenas. We had to go through the towns of La Palma and Blaidin. That seaport was very important as I have mentioned before. All kinds of business and passenger movements took place on that seaport. People used to travel to Naguabo, Humacao and Puerto Rico on vessels or motorized boats using that seaport. The trains moved merchandise to and fro from this seaport, using the rail tracks. Most of the goods were transported to Playa Grande before being distributed to the customers around the island.

There was another road to Punta Arenas from Mosquito through the mangroves of the Kiani and El Podre lagoons. The rail tracks from Martineau also reached Punta Arenas along the side of the roads.

Mosquito

Mosquito was another important seaport town for the people of Vieques. From this seaport passengers used to travel to the nearest ports in Puerto Rico like Ceiba and Naguabo. This town had a considerable population. There was a theater where they produced their own shows and community activities. It was in that theater that my mother saw the first silent movies of Charlie Chaplin and many others.

The seaports of Mosquito, La Esperanza, Punta Arenas and Puerto Mulas in Isabel Segunda were the spinal cord of a strong economy on Vieques Island.

At that time the population of Vieques comprised French, British, British Isles, Portuguese descendants, and the large group of Spanish people from Puerto Rico who followed the earlier French settlers. Spanish was the main language, followed by the British Isles' version of English. French had disappeared as the main spoken language although some French people still lived on the island.

The Life at El Sapo (The Line)

At this stage of our life on the route to our destiny, my mother and father continued being separated. My mother had six sons and daughters. A son and a daughter from a first marriage. Her first husband died just before their only son was born. After that she met my father and gave birth to three sons and a daughter. Guateen, who was the second son from that last marriage, was practically adopted by Don Diaz and Mrs. Dominga. Dominga was my mother's cousin. Alice, the older daughter, spent many days at Dominga's house helping out with the domestic tasks. Angel, my older brother, spent most of his time at his uncle Alexander's home. Alexander had no wife or sons. So Angel filled that gap in his life. My mother had to take care of Nestor, Yolanda and me. The four of us lived at aunt Juanita's house in the neighborhood of El Sapo. The place where we lived in this neighborhood had two lines of houses, one on each side of the road to Playa Grande. There were about ten houses on each side of the road. People usually called it "The Line" because the houses were lined up, parallel to each other. The houses were rustic houses, especially built for the technicians and locomotive engineers who worked for La Central. They were made with wood and roofed with metal sheets. The name of El Sapo came from the name of the brook to the east of us. There, the women used to wash clothes or do the necessary cleaning of household goods. There were two wells built on that brook from where people used to get the necessary water for bathing, cooking and other purposes. People used to collect rain water in drums by the side of the houses; that water came down from the roofs on rainy days. Either of both water sources was used to cook. The fuel used to cook was dried branches of mangrove, dried peels of coconuts, cachasa, charcoal or any dried piece of wood available.

Home cooked food consisted of fried fish with fried arepas; red kidney beans stewed with pork meat in a thick tomato sauce accompanied with baked arepas or rice; stewed fish in a thick tomato sauce with boiled white sweet potato; rice and beans with fried chicken or fried fish; boiled vegetables with cod fish salad; lobster or sea snails salads; lobster gumbo; crab meat rice; stewed crab meat and many others. But the most liked of all was cornmeal mush made with salt, water and lard accompanied with broth made out of the heads of fresh fish. It was so because it was said that this meal was the best aphrodisiac of them all.

To the south of us lived various families that depended on the lagoon for economic means. To the east lived Mrs. Locadi, a strong woman who used to talk with a loud voice and with an accent different from many others. She used to talk in syllables. She had three pretty daughters and many men walked around her house to catch a glimpse of those girls. There was one night when one youngster took his guitar and decided to serenade the youngest of the girls. He started his song that expressed how much he was suffering for her love and that his soul was sick and ailing for her love. When Mrs. Locadi heard the serenader, she opened the window, took an empty bottle, threw it to the singer and said, “If you are sick and ai-ling, what the heck are you do-ing out-doors in the mid-dle of the night?”

In her peculiar way of talking, the next day she was telling the people of the neighborhood, “And there was Ro-sen-do sere-na-ding my dau-ghter when I threw him a bo-ttle. The bo-ttle hit him on his back while he was ru-nning and he yelled Chee! Chee!”

That incident was the gossip of the day over the entire neighborhood. Like any small community with almost no news, every small incident is big news.

There was another case that happened to my uncle Juan. He also fell in love with one of Locadi’s daughters. Since he was very timid he hired a guitarist to serenade the girl. That night they went early enough to serenade the girl before going to bed. The guitarist started to play his guitar and without him even starting to sing the girl opened the window.

“There she is, Juan!” the guitarist said.

Juan took off and hid behind the bushes.

“Come on, Juan, there she is, say something to her!”

"I am scared, I can't talk," said Juan.

"Come on, Juan, don't be bashful, say something!"

"You say something, I am so scared that I can't even talk," said Juan.

At that time they decided to get out of the bushes and leave the place with no results, due to the bashfulness of my uncle Juan.

The next day, everybody was making fun of Juan. That became a gossip for years. "You say something, I am scared."

To the south of us lived Mrs. Librada Diaz. She was a sweet and pretty blue-eyed mature woman. She was the midwife of the entire neighborhood, who helped bring to life many souls on this western part of Vieques.

Close to us lived Amador, the engineer of locomotive No. 8. He drove the locomotive that moved in between La Hueca and Playa Grande. Due to the peculiar sound that the locomotive made on the tracks, the kids around called him Amador Bam Bam. Every afternoon when the kids saw him coming home, they followed him saying, "Amador Bam Bam, Amador Bam Bam," while moving their hips sideways, like dancing. He smiled and continued walking home, not paying much attention to the kids. All he wanted was to get home and rest from the arduous work of the day. Amador got married to one of my uncle's daughters and they had two children. The girl was called Titi and the boy's name was Luis. His wife died at a very young age and Uncle Lolo, the grandfather, took care of both kids.

Mrs. Paula Mamerto lived across the road, to the north. She was feared because she was the spiritual counselor, the foreteller or the witch of the neighborhood. She read the cards and performed many spiritual acts for people who wanted luck or just a curse against somebody for revenge or for punishment. The ones who visited her the most were young girls anxious to know who was going to marry them in the near future.

Uncle Sico

The Diaz brothers lived southeast of us. They had a banana plantation and their house was in the middle of that plantation. It was very rare to see them out of their plantation. They worked all day long. The customers had to go to them to get the bananas and other vegetables that they produced and harvested. Their plantation was on the northeast side, very close to the lagoon. The name of the proprietor was Sico and his brother was Negron. They were blue-eyed, white, short men who wore a hat, trousers tied up to the ankles, but no shoes. All of us knew Sico as Uncle Sico.

There is a sad incident involving Uncle Sico. It happened when he was working, cutting canes. The foreman in charge found Uncle Sico sitting on a rock in the middle of the farm. Uncle Sico was sharpening his machete in order to continue cutting canes. The foreman approached him on his horse and started saying nasty words to him. Uncle Sico continued filing his machete without even muttering a word. In those days the foremen were the only people allowed to carry a gun on their waist. They also carried a dagger and a long machete or sword hanging from their waist. They used that machete to blast them on the back of the workers to make them work more or faster. The workers were much abused. They were very obedient in order to avoid trouble and continue making a living, even at the expense of being abused. During those days workers had to work from dawn to dusk.

Realizing that Uncle Sico was not paying any attention to him, the foreman dismounted his horse, took off his machete and lifted it in the air with his right hand, ready to hit Uncle Sico on his back. Immediately, Uncle Sico stood up and, with his machete, cut the left leg of the foreman. When the foreman fell down, Uncle Sico continued cutting the body of the foreman. Many workers came running from the cane farm to assist the foreman by removing Uncle Sico from the top of him.

"My goodness! He chopped him off like meat for a stew!" said the workers.

Uncle Sico spent many years in jail and, when he got out, he returned to his farm. Once in there, he never talked to anybody and was never seen outside his farm. He used Negron, his brother, to do all the business needed outside his farm. People liked to go to his farm because he always gave away fresh vegetables and ripe bananas kept in an old barrel without charging any money.

The Lagoon

My older sister Alice was already a teenager. Tony, one of the sons of Mrs. Librada, was always walking around our house trying to attract her attention. His interest in her was noticeable. The way he looked at her announced his intentions.

One day, during the afternoon, he approached me and said, "Nello, would you like to go for a boat ride on the lagoon?"

"Oh yes, I've never been on the lagoon," I said.

"Well then, follow me."

We walked west on a path to the end of El Sapo and then turned south. To my right the baseball park was visible. Baseball was the favorite sport on Sundays, with two games being played; one in the morning and the other in the afternoon after lunch and a good rest.

We continued walking south until we reached the mangroves. There were various paths inside that muddy and smelly area. They were prepared with ground rocks to prevent feet from sinking into the mud. There were thousands of crab caves throughout the mangroves' muddy grounds. I saw many narrow boardwalks built straight from the mangroves' area to the waters of the lagoon. There were many boats tied up to those boardwalks. The boats were used for hunting and fishing. This lagoon was very important to the all residents living in the southwest part of the island. The people hunted migratory ducks as a sport, or either for sale or for cooking at home. Many migratory birds used the lagoon's mangroves to nest in at their specific periods of nesting. The wood that this lagoon provided was used to make houses or shacks for animals. It was also used as fuel in the homes. Around the mangroves, there were forests of coconut palm trees that were also important. The leaves of these palm trees were used for roofing rustic houses. There was another plant that grew in these swampy grounds called hinea. This plant had very thick leaves and was used for roofing.

Tony took me to one of the boardwalks where he had his family's boat. We got into the boat. He started rowing towards the east of the lagoon. In the meantime, I was looking at the birds that went down into the water, fishing with their beaks. Some flew around and went down fast. Others stood still on the water, waiting for a fish to pass by, and then moved into the water very quickly for its catch. Tony continued rowing and made a turn to the south and then to the west. He continued rowing by bordering the mangroves and right in the middle of the lagoon, at the south side of it, I saw an opening like a channel, where the ocean could be seen. There was a wooden bridge across that channel. I could see the waves on the beach coming in and out of the channel reaching the lagoon's main water body. That channel was known as the mouth of the lagoon and was built in order to prevent flooding of the north side area during the season of heavy rains. This way the lagoon was to keep a certain safe level of water in it by emptying the excess into the ocean. Since it was below sea level, the high tides brought sea water followed by lots of salt water fish into the lagoon. This was to the benefit of the fishermen, because fishing with nets was easier in the lagoon than in the open sea.

I couldn't tell the size of the lagoon because I was only a kid. To me it was immense. Tony rowed to the widest part of the lagoon to the west, then turned north and then east to the little pier or boardwalk. It was late afternoon. The colors in the sky turned pink and reflected in the mangroves. The mangrove leaves showed a mix of green, silver and pink. The silver like waters of the lagoon also turned pink. It was beautiful, beautiful as I had never seen before. The rows of the fishermen and hunters, the fishing birds, the singing birds in the mangroves produced a sound that I am not afraid of saying was almost silent. It produced an echo that vanished quickly. The sounds seemed to move along the top of the waters, get into the mangroves and vanish.

The ecology system of this lagoon was responsible for great economic activity in the region.

We reached the pier. Tony tied up the row boat and got out. He lifted me up and put me down. We walked to his house, not too far north.

"Who is this little boy?' asked his mother.

"He is Nello, the younger son of Paula. I took him for a ride on the lagoon," he said.

"It is late in the afternoon, you should take him back home right now, but first, let me give him an arepita for the road," she said.

Since it was so late I devoured the arepita in seconds. When we got home my mother looked worried.

"Where have you been?" she asked.

"I took a boat ride on the lagoon with Tony," I answered.

"Are both of you nuts? Don't you know how dangerous that lagoon is for kids?" she said.

She didn't say another word and got into the house. Tony walked back home and I walked to the nearest mango tree and sat on a rock under it. Then I started to think over and over about that first adventure on the lagoon.

That lagoon is beautiful, extremely beautiful, I thought. *Some day I will have my own boat to hunt and fish in it.*

The Rumors

Anyone could feel it in the atmosphere. There was a threat of expropriation on the western side of the island. People were talking about it. Some believed it, others didn't. But there was the Second World War and Hitler's threat. The rumors said that the United States armed forces were going to use the west part of this island as an ammunition storage area. They argued that this area was very safe for that purpose. Others didn't believe that. On the front page of the English newspaper, *Vieques Breeze*, a cartoon showed German planes bombing the entire island of Vieques. Moreover, after the Second World War was over, three German U-boats were found in the shallow waters around the island. They died probably because they got short on fuel and couldn't advance or simply because of engines or communication defects. It meant that the Germans knew very well what was going on in this island.

Many of the residents of this western area understood that Hitler's threat was very serious and very submissively accepted the idea of letting the armed forces take over the area.

Due to this situation, all schools in the area closed down. In order to attend school we had to walk to Puerto Real where there was schooling from the first to the ninth grade. The only high school on the island was located in town.

Expropriation was imminent. The demolition of buildings and houses was occurring. I saw how the bulldozers were tearing down the houses with all the personal belongings inside. People were forced to leave fast, otherwise they could lose everything. A rumor was spread that said that the US armed forces had the intention of removing all inhabitants to send them to an Indian reservation in Arizona. They planned to remove everybody, including the cemetery. The people called that movement "Operation Dracula".

Many people said, "Why are they treating us like that? We are

American citizens and the majority of us are of the same European background as they are."

Some argued, "It could be that our skin darkened by the burning sun of the tropics made us look different."

It was a terrible situation for those who had little means to make a living. Losing their jobs without any type of compensation was very serious. Extreme poverty on the island was a known fact. The local government started to lose a high source of income due to the termination of the operation of La Central. Thousands of indirect and direct jobs disappeared. People who had the means moved to the Virgin Islands, to Puerto Rico and to the United States. The ones who couldn't find a place to live in had to move in with relatives or friends or to Monte Santo where the U.S. navy provided land for some of the expropriated people.

The Route to School

I was seven years old. We were still living at El Sapo when I went to school for the first time. It was a long walk. I walked about four miles to the east from El Sapo to Puerto Real. I had to go through the neighborhoods of Playita, across the Andino's bridge, La Hueca, across Rio Urbano's bridge, the road going up the hills of Source and Don Jovo's, El Pilon and La Llave and, to the right, there was the school. Barefoot, and with a brown sombrero to protect me from the hot tropical sun, I walked to Barbosa school in Puerto Real.

The main building of the school was built following an earlier European style, made with wide brick walls, roofed and floored with lumber. It had four classrooms and a small library. In the middle of the building, beneath the floor, was the cistern of rain water. The opening used to take the water from the cistern, which was on one side of the main hallway close to the fourth grade classroom. A table on the side held two earthen jars, one on top of the other. The water taken from the cistern was poured into the top jar that had a small hole on the bottom and a paper filter on the hole. The bottom jar received the filtered water. The filtered water was used for drinking and for cooking in the school's dining room. We drank the water using a custom made school-paper cup. The dining room was located in a building south of the main school building. The cooks were Mrs. Leonci and Mrs. Virginia. In between the school and the dining room was the first grade room. This one was built with wood and metal sheets. It was a spacious place, very comfortable for all activities carried out for the first graders. Our first grade teacher was Miss Gittings. She was a black woman who came from one of the British Isles in the Caribbean and settled in Vieques. She was very sharp, strict and showed pride in whatever she did. She could speak perfectly the Spanish Castilian language, the British English and the British Isles' English dialects. She was very aggressive and all mistakes were punishable. I was terribly afraid of her like all the kids. She could hit anybody with whatever she had on hand; a book, a chalkboard eraser, a ruler and even a shoe if there was nothing else close to her. She scared me every time she showed anger for some kid's mistake. She opened those red eyes and looked very ferocious coming to the kid to punish him. Once she ran towards me and I stood up from my seat and ran outdoors under a heavy rain. There were two girls with an umbrella close by the main building. I immediately hid in between the two girls when I saw Miss Gittings trying to grab my hands.

"Come on, baby, I am not going to hurt you," she said.

She laughed, and took me by my arms and returned to school. We got back to the room, all wet due to the heavy rain. She tried to calm me, but no matter what she did I was still frightened.

One day she started an arts class. She placed on the board a map of an island and on the chalkboard she made a rectangular figure. She asked us to draw that figure as best as we could. I didn't follow her instructions and drew the map of the island almost as perfectly as I saw it in the picture. When I turned my work in, she opened her eyes in surprise, showing the drawing to the class. She asked the rest of kids to stand up and give me an ovation.

After the first day of school was over, we started on our way back home. It was a very painful walk. I had never walked so far. The heat from the paved road hurt my feet and I felt that the pain moved all the way up to my knees. When I got home my mother came to me and asked, "How was that first day in school?"

"Ouch, look at my feet!" I said.

"What happened?" she asked.

"My feet hurt a lot!" I yelled.

When my mother looked at my feet, they were bleeding. I saw her eyes filling up with tears. She didn't talk for a while, and after a while she came to me and said, "Wait for me, in a moment I'll go to Playa Grande to get you something."

Getting bloody feet was normal for almost everybody who walked barefoot, but I was only a kid for such a long walk. So my mother went to Playa Grande to Manolo's store and bought me a pair of sneakers.

"The shoes are only to be used to go to school. When you come back from school, you take them off, put them aside on the corner of the room," she told me.

"Okay, Mom, thanks."

The next day's walk was not that painful, but my feet hurt and I felt pain at the end of the walk. The pain faded after getting used to those daily long walks.

To resist pain either physically or mentally, with patience and perseverance until it vanishes, could be considered a human virtue. This condition has to be developed at an early age. It could be considered as cruel, but if anybody does not learn how to persevere in difficult situations, no strong personalities could be developed in their route to mental and physical progress. Nobody has to be taught to be too dependent or weak, or to be excessively protected by groups or laws. This will lead to an attitude of "I will do whatsoever I please because there is someone or some law that will take me out of the situation". If the course of individual responsibility is not taken, we create selfish attitudes of "Give me, go on, and forget about it". There are ancient and modern organizations that promote certain types of attitudes and they don't realize that they are creating weak and prejudiced minds. From those attitudes they develop suicide acts, confrontations, confusions and finally repentance.

La Hueca

The news was all over the island. The United States was already committed with other European nations to fight against Hitler. Now, the people moving out of the western side knew that there was no way back on the expropriation process. We had reached the point of no return. The United States had already joined forces with England and French people to liberate France from the Nazis and to defeat Hitler's forces. People continued to move out. Men with wheelbarrows loaded with things, women with bundles over their heads and tears in their eyes, were seen moving to the east in a hurry.

Rationing of food started to affect everybody. The prices of goods started to rise. That situation made our life quite uncomfortable. The provisions that we could get were either of bad quality or very old. People noticed it because of the strange smell that emanated from them.

My mother and the children were forced to leave aunt Juanita's house because they were to move to San Juan in Puerto Rico.

Now we had to follow a route to God knows where.

We continued along the routes as situations appeared without a definite path. We never established a definite goal. We struggled for survival without planning for the future. The route was going to take us to unexpected places, through an unknown path.

My mother finally got a house up the road in La Hueca. It was a wooden house with metal sheets on the roof. It had a concrete stairway from the house to the main road.

On a very dark Friday night we moved to the new house. It had to be on a Friday because my brothers and myself were attending school and we needed time the next day to organize the house. In two trips we moved everything. We used a cart with a kerosene lantern in front of it. My two brothers and I helped mother move everything in.

The next day I woke up early and got out of the house in a hurry. I had seen the place before on my route to school, but the curiosity of a child to learn more and more about the places made me get up early to walk around the place. To the west of us, there was a house painted blue and red and in the backyard of that house there was a garden of tropical fruits. Many trees of a large variety of tropical fruits had been planted there. I saw mango trees, quenepa, apreen, algarrobo and many others. To the east, down the road, there was a grocery store that belonged to the Velez-Diaz family. To the south, there were few farms with sugarcane plantations, and across the road to the very south of us, a cattle farm with its green pastures. This one was a dairy farm. Our house was located on the slope of a small hill from where we could enjoy watching the Caribbean Sea in all its splendor. Farther to the east, we could see the pier of La Esperanza seaport, with the two winches on the quay and the two keys out in the sea. From our house I enjoyed watching the different types of vessels moving in a zigzag pattern, taking advantage of the direction of the wind to move along. The bigger boats, with three or four masts, carried loads of merchandise to other Caribbean islands and the smaller boats were of local merchants or fishermen. Out in the sea, about a mile from the coast there were two buoys, one red and the other black for alerting sailors that there was danger from emerging rocks or shallow waters in that specific place.

On the farms to the south were the houses of Gene Velez and Don Diaz, right in the middle of their sugarcane fields.

The land where our house was located was a lot from the original French settlers, the Monets, of whom my mother was a descendant. That land went to other peoples' hands in a mysterious way, leaving many of the Monets with nothing.

There was pasture going up the hill at the back of our house. My mother took advantage of that and started raising chickens, goats and pigs on a limited scale because the property was not ours.

A man called Don Santo came periodically to buy our eggs. He was always accompanied by his retarded son, Fito. Fito was always barefoot and ran besides Don Santos, always holding the mare as they moved along from place to place.

I remember the first time I was punished by my mother. I had heard many words from kids in school and other men talking to each other, but never understood many of them. So, one day when Don Santo was approaching our house, I stood up and said some of those words to him.

"What are you saying, boy?" asked Don Santo, very surprised.

"I said what I said, didn't you like it?"

When my mother heard that expression, she grabbed my arm, lifted me up and hit me several times on my butt.

"Take this, and this, and this, you ought to be respectful to all people!"

Down to the south of us, we had the favorite beach of the neighborhood. It was named the Pass of the Boats. It was a small beach with tranquil waters and very safe. Out in the sea, surrounding this beach, there were coral reefs that didn't allow big fishes like sharks or barracudas to get in. It had a shallow opening on the reefs to the southeast that allowed the fishermen's boats to get in and out. For that reason it was named the Pass of the Boats.

Every time we wanted to swim, groups of kids and older people went down to the Pass. We caught fish and lobsters on the beach, using spears or sharp machetes and cooked them on a fire made with dry branches of the sea grape bush in between four rocks.

To the west of the beach lived Marcial with his wife and three daughters. He had an ancient record player that had to be wound up manually in order to play. He was the only person in the whole place around who had one of these. We used to go to his home on some afternoons to listen to the music on the records he had. There were no radio receivers in the neighborhood during those days, so "record playing" at Marcial's home was the only mechanical or electrical means of entertainment in that area. His house was located at the edge of a small hill by the beach and very close to Andino's brook.

Belford was a farm worker and fisherman who fell in love with the older of Marcial's daughters. Later, he married her. Belford built a house close to and to the west side of Marcials'. They lived close together and looked for work, one always following the other.

To the north and close to the main road lived Tony Cigar. He was the man in charge of maintaining a section of the main road in good traveling conditions. He had to cover a section of road of about five miles from the Mine to Andino. He worked with a big cigar in his mouth. He was a guitarist. For all activities where a musician was needed, Tony Cigar was there with his group.

To the north of Tony's home there was a hill where there was a rock on top of another named the Mounted Rock. It was a huge mass, almost spherical. Many times I climbed up that rock with the help of other kids in order to watch the area around. Going downhill from the Mounted Rock, there was a cave on the ground. People around said that in ancient times there was a ghost named El Yure, whose favorite place to hide was the Mounted Rock and that cave. The ghost used to run down the hill close to midnight with a loud and infernal sound, covered in a dense black cloud to chase people and take away all they had on them, including clothes. He covered the victims with that cloud to make them unable to see or hear anything. When he left, the people continued with the cloud covering them for some time until the Yure had disappeared. I was told that the Yure was mostly seen on roads where there was a hill overlooking them, and always before midnight. The people in the neighborhood used to scare kids at nights by saying, "Run for your life, the Yure is coming!"

To the west of the Mounted Rock lived Martina and Nicasio. Martina was a pretty woman who had two white-haired, blue-eyed beautiful girls. She had some sort of bad reputation and most of the women around never talked to her. Her home was the place of entertainment at weekends for many men who lived around. Men used to bring gallons of rum to her house. They gave enough rum to her husband Nicasio until he got dead drunk. At this point started the orgy with Martina and her two daughters.

"Martina for God Martina,
Martina, Queen of my heart,
Before Nicasio wakes up
Give me more and more rum."

The men used to sing in chorus, and the party continued all night long until dawn.

On various occasions, my brother Nestor went with our uncles to Martina's. My mother always advised him not to eat anything in that house.

"Don't you dare eat anything in that place, I am warning you!"

My brother never took the advice and, since my mother was not present, he ate whatever Martina gave him. After he got back my mother asked him, "What did you eat in that house?"

"Nothing, there was nothing to eat," he answered.

"I don't believe you. Come here, I will give you something to throw up whatever you ate."

It was a terrible situation for my brother because my mother's medicine was a lot worse than Martina's food.

After Nicasio's death, and in her late years, Martina dedicated herself to working as a spiritual counselor. And after her death, her younger daughter got married and lived in the same house for years with her husband, Gavino. She had only one son by the name of Gene. The other daughter got married also, but left to some unknown place. Some people said that she went to Chicago with her husband.

One thing that called my attention in this new place was the kids playing "wheel and the garapeen". I saw them running after the wheel and I was anxious to do the same. The favorite wheel was the band that held the middle part of the barrel. The garapeen was a hand-made hook to guide the wheel. It was made with a strand of the barbed wire cable. That piece of wire was very strong and difficult to bend. The grocery store of the Diaz-Velez family used to throw away a barrel when worn out and not in use. This being the case, I was always looking for an opportunity to grab one and remove the wheel from it, to start running alongside the other kids. A time came when I was able to satisfy my wishes.

Dominga's Farm

Ever since we lived at El Sapo, almost every Sunday we went to visit Dominga, my mother's cousin. Guateen, my brother, lived with her because she never had a son. She decided to take care of him and it was to the advantage of my mother who had to support all her children on her own. Her husband was Don Diaz, a retired policeman. He retired because of health problems after a stomach operation. They said that half of his stomach was removed and the doctors told him to retire and rest until his death. In the many places where he worked as a policeman in Puerto Rico they called him "Candelita". That means "the hot one" or "pure fire". They lived on Dominga's farm. She inherited seven acres of land from her father, Bernardino Monet. The farm extended to the south, from the main road to the beach. It was an almost plain terrain with a slight slope down to the sea. At the very end of the farm, on the sands of the beach, was a forest of palm trees, a very tall almond tree and a fresh water pond coming from the brook to the west of the farm. That pond was full of toads and tiny fresh water fishes that made it very interesting to watch. Along the brook there was a palm tree that had many leaves very close to one other, making it very difficult to climb on it.

One day Marcial came with Belford to get all the dry coconuts from that palm tree. Belford climbed up the palm and got stuck in between the leaves. He yelled to Marcial, "Marcial, I'm falling!"

"No, don't fall yet, hold it, let me remove some stakes from underneath!" said Marcial.

"Damn it, Marcial, I can't hold from nowhere, my arms are stuck! I am sliding down!" said Belford.

"I am telling you to hold on and don't fall yet. I still have to remove some barbed wire!" Marcial insisted.

"Damn it, Marcial, it isn't that I want to fall, it is that I am fa-a-a-a-lling! Marciaaaaal!"

And down he went to the ground, sliding down the leaves

with the good luck that Marcial had already removed the barbed wire.

"See, I told you to hold it," said Marcial.

"To hold it, to hold it. As if it was that easy," said Belford. "Now you climb up and go for the coconuts"

They sat down for a while and later on Belford tried successfully. Marcial was an aged person and had no energy to climb up a palm tree.

Don Diaz and Dominga were persons very important for our family and also for the entire neighborhood. They were not greedy people and very serviceable. They gave away whatever anybody needed, for nothing in exchange.

My mother and Alice, my older sister, liked to help Dominga with the domestic tasks. Nestor, Guateen and I helped Don Diaz with the farm works, including putting up barbed wire fences.

Don Diaz had two daughters from a previous marriage. Genoveve, the younger one, spent her younger years in Vieques with her father, and during the Second World War she joined the Women's Army Corps (WACS). When the war was over she went to New York, attended and graduated from university. There she married an Italian fashion designer. They moved to Vieques at retirement age and built a little mansion by the beach at La Esperanza. That house has a magnificent view of La Esperanza seaport and the quays. The house has a balcony in each room facing the sea.

The older of the daughters of Don Diaz married a person from Wisconsin and lived there for the rest of her life. After the Second World War was over, she traveled all the way from Wisconsin to spend a few days with her father. She had two teenage daughters who couldn't speak Spanish. Don Diaz, their grandfather, couldn't speak English. It was a very sad situation and funny at the same time to watch the granddaughters and their grandpa trying to talk to each other. He tried hard to understand what was going on. All he did was embrace the young girls and laugh in his own peculiar way.

"Ha, ha, ha!"

Dominga's farm was located between the farms of Velez-Diaz on the western side and Catalina's farm on the eastern side. It had a pathway coming from the main road on the north leading to the beach on the south. In the middle of the farm, not too far from the beach, they built the house. It had three bedrooms, a living room, a dining room, a balcony on the northern side overlooking the west, a kitchen in a little house to the south, and a cistern of rain water at the eastern side of the kitchen. The cistern was made with concrete in a rectangular hole in the ground. It had a series of gutters on the sides of the roof to get the rain water straight down. It could hold at least one thousand gallons of rain water. This water was used for all the needs in the house: drinking, cooking bathing and cleaning. There was a small hallway between the house and the kitchen. It was roofed to prevent the rain water from getting into either the kitchen or the house. There was a wooden stairway on the western side of the hallway that served as the entrance to both the house and the kitchen.

In the evenings, after a long day's work, Don Diaz used to sit on his rocking chair on the balcony, put both his hands on the back of his head and started daydreaming. With a tasty Chesterfield cigarette lit between his lips sending smoke to the air, looking west towards a colorful sunset, I heard him say, "I wish I had five hundred thousand millions of dollars. Ha, ha, ha!"

Then he started to recite his favorite poems.

Then he said, "There is nothing better than a good day's work, a delicious meal, and after a fresh bath, get into bed with a strong and pretty woman. Ha, ha, ha!"

Then he continued reciting his favorite poems and smoking his Chesterfield, his favorite cigarette.

On the western side of the house he built a smaller house to keep his farm tools and other equipment used on the farm. Close to this little house he had a home-made distillery to make rum from the molasses he bought from the sugar mill. In that shack he also stored the charcoal used for the kitchen and the distillery.

Don Diaz's room was the one to the south of the house. The room had a door to the cistern, looking south towards the beach. He always left the door half open at nights when in bed to watch the cattle. He kept his cattle in place by the ridge, at the end of the farm. He had a 38-caliber long barrel revolver always under his pillow. On many nights he got up after midnight, shooting in the air and chasing away the little gray people who were molesting his cows. The little gray people ran down the ridge to the beach and disappeared.

Dominga's room was in the middle room of the house. It was well decorated with a very luxurious wooden bed, a dresser, night stands, cabinets, wardrobe and a carpeted floor. The room's furniture looked shiny and well placed.

There was a smaller room in the northern part of the house. This room was used as the guests' room. Guateen, my brother, had his bed in Don Diaz's room.

To the east of the house, Don Diaz built the hurricane refuge. This was a small pyramidal low shack, made out of palm tree leaves and trunks. It could accommodate about ten people. It was so low that nobody could stand up inside it. For some time two fishermen lived in that shack. Their names were Loi and Viro. They worked on their nets and on their fish traps all day long at the Pass of the Boats, then came to sleep, late in the evening. On Wednesdays, they used to go and lift the fish traps, get their catch, and go out to sell them. One of the curious things that I observed was that the lobsters they caught were used as bait to catch fish. They cut them into small pieces and placed the pieces inside the fish traps.

Dominga never charged any money from these people to live in that shack, but she was always the first to check on the catch and ask for the best fish she could get. They had to leave the place because Dominga got tired of them. On Saturdays, they used to go to La Esperanza, get drunk and late at night come down the pathway singing and making lots of noises. That was the end of their easy life.

There were two small brooks at the farm. There was one that was close to the Velez-Diazs' and the other was in the middle of the farm, looking down from the house. At the end of this brook, Don Diaz used trunks of palm trees to build a small trough. He built it just at the end of the farm and before the beach. The trough was used to trap the water for his cattle and horses. There were few palm trees in this area, up the slope of a small hill. He also made a well at the beginning of the stream that formed the brook. The water of this well was used to bathe the animals, mostly the horses.

Most of the farmland was located to the north of the house. The railway path was right in the middle of the farm and across it. He had sugarcane on the northern and southern side of the railways. The vegetables were grown in a small site south of the house where the soil was always wet and very fertile.

Dominga was an expert cook. Her way of seasoning food was something special. Everything she cooked had a delicious taste, seasoned expertly. Her stews were unique. She used to cook stews with all kids of meats, either pork, chicken, beef, turkey, goat and whatsoever. It could have been that she learned from her mother the French fricassee style of cooking. She made cheese with the leftover milk. She prepared the milk by removing the serum, made a paste like dough, then after a day, she formed that dough in a round mold made of cowhide. She wrapped it up with banana leaves and buried it in the ground for several days. After several days, she unburied the cheese and put it in the center of the dinette table in the kitchen for consumption. She called her cheese "ground cheese".

She also made great cakes. The cake mix she made was placed on a mold and the mold placed inside a pot. This pot was put on top of a grill with lit charcoal. She put a sheet of metal on top of the pot and covered it with lit charcoal. In that manner she figured out how to make a home-made oven.

All days of the year, year after year, work on that farm seemed to have no end. There was something to do at every moment of the day.

Don Diaz got up early in the morning, around four thirty, to milk the cows and the goats, fill in all the containers for the people who bought milk from him. After that, he took his machete and hoe and walked to his farm plantations to the north. There he had sugarcane, corn and many other vegetables for home use.

He got back by noon for lunch and a little rest. Then, in the afternoon, he went back to the plantations to continue his farm work.

They raised chicken, guinea fowls, goats, pigs, cattle and had a mare and a horse. He rented some nearby pasture farms for his cattle. On afternoons, we had to move the cattle back to his farm and to the site by the edge of the ridge.

Dominga took care of feeding the chickens, the guinea fowls and the pigs. She was in charge of watching the distillery when in operation, and the general cleaning of the surroundings of the house.

She always needed extra help for all the work in the house. That is why my older sister spent many of her younger years at Dominga's house. Of all the farms around, this one was the most productive of them all.

Ever since we lived at El Sapo my sister Alice lived and worked in Dominga's house, always helping her to alleviate the heavy load of household work. After my sister graduated from eighth grade she moved to San Juan' to one of her sisters from her father's side. She moved there in the hope of getting a better way of life. She was an adolescent. I don't know what happened but she only spent a few months there and came back home. Genoveve had joined the WACS and my sister joined Dominga again.

Various people visited Don Diaz's house, especially on Sundays. They came either to enjoy a good fricassee or to get enough rum for the week.

Don Manolo, one of the store owners in Playa Grande, came on a Sunday. He parked his Ford Wagon close to a slope in the southern part of the yard. My brother Guateen, who was a mischievous kid, said to me, "I am going to show you that I am as strong as Superman."

"You are nuts," I told him.

"Oh yeah? Now look at me."

Guateen tried to push the car down the slope but couldn't move it.

"Just help me push a little bit, let me alone and you will see," he said.

I pushed a little, and the car started to move downhill. When we realized that there could be danger, we ran downhill as fast as we could, went through three fences of barbed wire, ran across Catalina's farm and slid down the ridge, to the sands of the beach below. We looked at each other with our eyes wide open showing how frightened we were.

"Wow, what a shock!" Guateen said.

"What shock, aren't you Superman?" I said.

"What are we going to do now?" he asked.

"Well, let us move uphill and see what is going on up there," I said.

We climbed up the hill, showing a bit of our little heads over the border of the ridge. We noted that the car had stopped on a tree just in front of it. It didn't seem to have any damage. We stood there watching until one man came out of the distillery's shack and said, "Hey, Manolo, your car went downhill."

Don Manolo came out of the shack, looked at the car and said, "Oh my God, I probably left it too close to the slope. Please, help me push it back up the hill."

We got out of this one. Luckily, nobody had seen us pushing the car downhill.

Dominga's house was a shopping place for the neighborhood. Periodically, she received the Sears Roebuck and Company mail order catalog from Chicago. Women and men got together to fill in orders for the goods needed. They ordered housewares in general. Don Diaz ordered leather boots, cowboy hats, jeans and whatever he needed for himself and for farm work. He ordered the first radio receiver in the neighborhood. It was a Silvertone radio operated with a direct current battery. The battery lasted for about six months. He was aware of that and every fifth month he ordered a Silvertone radio battery from Sears. The radio operated with a stranded copper wire antenna, about sixty feet long, with glass insulators at each end. He installed the antenna on a pole from the side of the house to the farthest side of the tool house to the west. It also had to be grounded. He installed the true ground copper wire from the back of the radio through a hole in the floor, put a four-inch nail at the end of the wire and hammered it into the ground underneath the floor of the house. He placed the radio on a shelf between the living and the dining room. Many people from the neighborhood came during the evenings to listen to soap operas, the news and some music. For some period of time Dominga's house was a center of entertainment, until Bartolo bought a similar radio receiver from Sears Roebuck and

Company. Sears, a very efficient company, sent all products as ordered and within the expected time. People loved to order products from Sears. Products were neatly packaged and shipped via U.S. Parcel Post and received a month after ordered. That was a very good delivery time, considering the annoying delays due to transportation problems in those days.

We spent many evenings with my sister Alice on the ridge near the beach, at Dominga's farm. She sat on the border of that low cliff and sung as many songs she could, with the accompaniment of the sounds of the sea waves and breeze. She liked to sing South American waltzes and tangos. We liked to sit there at sunset to make it more romantic.

Right in that area we celebrated the day of La Candelaria, which meant the fire day. On the second day of February Don Diaz built a wooden frame about four feet wide and about twenty feet high. He covered it with dried palm tree leaves. As soon as it got dark on that day, he set fire to that tower and all of us kids danced, sang and yelled to Saint Blas of the Candelaria on and on until the fire extinguished. Don Diaz loved to see us kids having fun on that evening.

"Ha, ha, ha!" He laughed repeatedly.

Alice was always daydreaming and thinking about the man of her dreams. She said that she was going to marry a white, blue-eyed man. Her dreams came true because, later in her life, she married Librada's son, Tony, who was a blue-eyed, white man.

The Beating

I could never forget the beating. On one of those Sundays that we visited the house of Dominga, and while I was eating lunch, Don Diaz came up the stairway and into the kitchen, very furious and with a rope on his hand. Immediately, he started beating me from side to side on my arms, on my back, on my thighs, on my head, over my whole body.

"Take this, and this, and this, you scoundrel, you've got to learn from this!"

He continued beating me to the point that I couldn't feel any pain anymore. My mother, watching and realizing that she couldn't prevent it, put her hands over her head, started to scream, ran over the cistern and fell down under an almond tree. Laying on the ground, she continued screaming. Don Diaz looked out the door and saw my mother on the ground and heard her screaming. At this point he stopped beating me and asked, "What is going on, why is Paula screaming?"

At that instant, I ran to my mother who was still laying on the ground. She embraced me and both of us continued crying. Dominga came over to help my mother get up. She looked at my body all beaten up with all sorts of bruises. After we got up my mother took her things, and my little sister in a hurry. We walked back home without saying a word.

I really don't know why that strong man didn't kill me that day. He was a very rustic man, over six feet tall with all the strength that anyone could imagine. When we got home, I asked my mother, "Why did he beat me, Mom?"

"I don't know, baby, he was dead drunk," she answered.

My mother immediately put lots of grease on all my bruises and asked me to lay in bed until I felt better. The skin all over my body looked awful. I couldn't believe anybody could deserve such a beating, especially a seven-year-old child who never did anything extremely wrong.

The next day, very early in the morning I heard a conversation outdoors.

"How is the boy?"

"He is in bed with fever, his whole body is hurt and painful, this has been a disaster for that little kid."

"I am really sorry, I want you and the baby to forgive me, I don't remember doing anything. Dominga told me about it and I couldn't believe what I heard. Please forgive me, for God's sake!"

That was the end of the conversation. Being a religious woman, my mother forgave Don Diaz and after that incident everything continued in a normal way. I couldn't attend school for few days until the swelling went down.

At Dominga's, I learned how to read at a very early age. Every Sunday, Don Diaz used to go to town on his mare to sell eggs and vegetables. He always bought the Sunday newspaper. I liked to look at the cartoons section. So I asked my sister to tell me what the characters were saying. She started to show me how to read. I learned quickly and could enjoy reading *Buck Rogers*, *The Phantom*, *Henry*, *Mandrake the Magician* and others. Those Sundays were very important to me and helped me in my education.

The Velez-Diaz

Close to our house, to the east of the road lived the Velez-Diaz family. Natalio, the older of the brothers, moved to town after making a fortune from the farm and the grocery store. Berto, his brother, took over the store. While in town, Natalio founded a theater and a hotel and bought another store. Both the theater and the hotel were named after his daughter, Violeta.

The grocery store at La Hueca was a smelly place. You could smell the dried codfish, the pigs' feet and mackerel kept in brine inside a barrel, the old smelly cheese and other smelly products. There were no freezers those days, and almost every perishable product had to be salted for preservation. His other brother, Jose, established a garment and fabrics store on the eastern side of the grocery store and very close to it.

Later in the years, Natalio and Berto hit the first prize of the Puerto Rican lottery. For this reason, Natalio let Berto take over his store in town. Berto moved to town and turned in the grocery store at La Hueca to his younger brother, Gene.

The Vanishing Corpse

A rare incident took place during the early years of my life. One of our neighbors passed away. He lived alone and he had nobody to take care of him, even when he was alive. My uncles decided to take care of his burial. They looked over for some lumber to make a coffin and a frame to carry the coffin to the cemetery in town. During the afternoon of that day, they decided to start their way towards town. On the way, they stopped in a road store and bought a gallon of rum. They had to stop during their trip for a rest and every time they stopped they had a shot of rum and a short conversation to minimize the burden. Just before reaching town, on a dark evening, they stopped by a place where there were a group of trees called the Higueros and put the coffin down. They were so distracted on their way that they didn't realize that for a long distance they were carrying an empty coffin. When they lifted the coffin up, they felt that it was too light. They looked into the coffin and found out that it was empty, that the corpse and the bottom part of the coffin had vanished. In the beginning they thought that the Higueros had stolen the corpse because the many legends about the disappearances of people in that area. But since they were almost drunk, they mustered up some courage, forgot all about legends and decided to walk back and look for the corpse, down the road. They kept walking back, looking for the corpse, until they found it in a trench on the side of the road, by the neighborhood of the Mine. They looked for a hammer in this place to repair the broken coffin, put the corpse back into it and continued their way to the cemetery. They finally made it close to midnight. Since it was late at night they spent the rest of it at El Canon.

The Mine neighborhood was named as such because the earlier French settlers exploited a copper mine in this area.

The Expropriation

At this time the U.S. navy had acquired the eastern part of Vieques and the airport site on Puerto Ferro was closed to civilians. Many people had abandoned the west and the population of the island was diminishing drastically. The railroad stopped operating. All the sugarcane bales had to be transported on trucks to the sugar mill.

The magazines and the causeway of Mosquito were in the process of being built. They hired civilians to help build them. Most of the magazines were built underground for security and safety purposes. Most of the hills in the west were dug out for this purpose.

La Central continued its operation until government authorities could figure out what to do with all the farming on the island. After the shutting down of La Central, the government decided to transport the sugarcane bales in barges to Pasto Viejo in Humacao. They used the seaport of La Esperanza to load the barges.

The navy installed a cable across the road between Andino and La Hueca, from a tree to a fence pole. It was located on the road right at the place where the Yure showed up the most, down below the Mounted Rock. This was a checkpoint where everybody, including pedestrians, passenger cars and buses, had to stop and be checked for identification. The residents of Vieques had to go to an office in Mosquito to apply and get a pass and an identification card. At this checkpoint, people were not allowed to go on without identification.

Many residents couldn't believe that strangers from other places treated us as strangers on our own land. They could drive and walk around the island freely, but the people who were residents, who were born and had lived in Vieques forever, were treated like enemies. Some people asked, "Are we members of the Nazi forces?"

In order to go to town we had to take a bus whose route was from town to Puerto Real, to La Hueca, Playa Grande, Mosquito and finally to town. That route never changed until the navy finally closed down the west area forever. Later on, the U.S. navy built a fence from north to south from Mosquito to Playita, just a few feet east off the end of the lagoon.

My mother used to go to town almost every month to visit her godmother. Her godmother was in charge of a mansion belonging to a very rich farmer. It was a very richly decorated mansion. The preferred color was light blue. Most of the mansion was painted blue and the floor was also carpeted in blue. Decorations included many oil paintings and natural flowers from the mansion's gardens. My mother's godmother took care of those details.

Coming Back from School

Bartolo and Paita bought the property where we lived and of course we had to move again. They moved to the bigger house on the western side of us. They had a son named Pango. Pango was a fearful and nervous boy. A little skinny black boy who lived in Playa Grande learned about that while in school. Every afternoon, the little boy hid behind a tree on the road and waited for Pango. When Pango was walking by, the skinny black boy suddenly jumped in front of him. Right there, we started to have fun when the chase began. Pango ran and the little boy chased him for a moment. The boy stopped chasing Pango and hid behind a tree. Pango looked back and, not seeing the boy, he also stopped running. The boy then jumped over the barbed wire fences and without being seen by Pango ran through the sugarcane fields or pastures to get ahead on the road and wait for Pango again. Hidden behind a tree, he suddenly stepped in front of Pango again and the chase started all over again. For us kids that was lots of fun on our way back home because when the chase started we also ran after Pango and the kid.

Coming back home from school, on many occasions I liked to walk alone. I liked to stay away from other kids in order to keep my mind busy daydreaming and to think clearly, with no distractions. It happened that downhill on Source there lived Remigio and his sons. The sons of Remigio waited by their home with a pile of rocks. Every time they saw me walking alone, they threw rocks on me. It was really painful when one of those rocks hit me on my legs and on my back. The only thing I could do was to run for my life. While in school, I mentioned that situation to one of my friends.

"Boy, this is terrible, every time I walk alone those kids throw rocks on me. I always look around before passing by, but they hide somewhere in the house and get out suddenly to throw those rocks," I said.

"Look, there is another path that you can take and they will never see you," he advised.

"But, where is it?" I asked.

"Look, when you pass Don Jovo's brook take a left to the path between the cane fields and walk straight down south until you find the road to La Esperanza. There you take a right and right there you are on your way home, without being disturbed."

That I did when I wanted to walk alone. Some time later, the boys approached me in school and said, "We haven't seen you for days walking back home."

"My family moved out to another place," I said.

They walked away, saying nothing. I continued walking down that route until they had forgotten all about it.

We Moved

As I said before, the house where we lived was sold and we had to move again. Not too far down the road, to the east, there was an empty house where we moved. That house had five bedrooms, a big living room a dining room and, of course, the house of the kitchen and a big spherical steel tank for rain water. It was customary to build a house for cooking separate from the main house for safety purposes. In that house we took the three bedrooms to the east and the kitchen. The rooms to the west were taken by Sadoc and his wife, a recently married young couple. We shared the balcony, the living room and the kitchen. The balcony covered the whole front of the house, looking towards and not too far from the main road. Right in front of the balcony we had mango trees that provided us with a nice shade in the afternoons. We liked to sit in our rocking chair on the balcony and rest well with the fresh breeze blowing from the sea. Like all kids, curiosity led me to climb up to the ceiling above the living room. It was all covered with dust and lint, probably accumulated for decades. Digging into that dusty area, I found various portraits of elegant men and women. Men with thick mustaches, well dressed in ancient European-style suits. Pretty women with dresses up to the neck and hairdos also European. I asked about those people but nobody remembered anyone like them. They were probably the original owners of that ancient house. It seemed that far back in time, and after their death, their descendants put those portraits there and forgot to remove them or just left them in there forever.

To the north, east and west there were sugarcane fields. To the north side of the backyard, there was a line of mango trees and to the west there was a small tree that produced a perfumed pod. The dry pods were used in the closets to let them add a good smell to the clothes. The tree was named hilan-hilan. In this place there were some tropical fruit trees like pomegranates and others.

My mother used the northern part of the backyard to raise

pigs, chicken and goats, the ones we had moved from our previous dwelling.

Far to the north, by the slope of Adon's hill, Don Guille had a plantation of sesame seeds.

Across the road was the farm of Catalina. Not to far to the west was the entrance to her house. The entrance had a garden of flower plants on both sides that made it look very pretty. Very close to her house, she also had a garden of tropical fruits. This garden of fruits was the largest in this neighborhood. There were many varieties of fruits in about half an acre of land. Mango trees were the dominant ones because it was the favorite fruit. Mangoes of many different sizes and varied taste were all over the place.

I was still attending my first grade of school until graduation. Our graduation was celebrated in the same first grade room at Barbosa school. Our uniform for graduation was all white. Boys had to wear white suits with a carnation on the left side pocket of the suit. Shoes and socks also had to be white. The girls, with a curly hairdo, wore brand new beautiful white dresses with white shoes and socks. They wore a corsage with red flowers.

The graduation went on, with all the regular ceremonies like dedications, speeches, songs, poems and at last the delivery of diplomas.

Balbina

On the road in front of our house, many things happened while we lived in that area. One of people who impressed me the most was an old white skinny and tall woman named Balbina. She had very long white hair. She used to wear a long dress and had a white mare to move her from place to place. She looked like a scary ugly old witch like those in the horror movies.

Every time she passed down the road in front of our house, she got off the mare and started talking loud and hitting that beast with a club. Then she climbed up on the neck of the animal and bit it several times in the neck with extreme ferocity. Then she got off again and continued beating the beast with the club. The beast stood up on its rear legs and jumped up from side to side, looking down at that mad woman with its eyes wide open. That was a real terror show. I was terrorized every time that woman stopped by my house. She probably knew that she scared the hell out of me because every time she approached my house she stopped and enacted the same terror show. Extremely terrorized, and hiding underneath the floor of the house, I kneeled down to watch that show. Some time later in my life, I learned that the woman was brought from Brazil to work as a servant. Don Antonio brought her on one of his trips to South America. She cracked up and went to live with another crazy fellow by the name of Majeron. They lived in Source in a little shack made of old metal sheets. The house was so low that they walked inside the house in a kneeling position. They were the poorest ones in the whole region. They ate whatever they could find in the neighborhood and around them. They had no furniture and they sat and slept over old sacks. Since they were so poor and crazy, most of the people around made fun of them. They had no help from anybody. Under those living conditions, they had two daughters and a son. The older daughter became mentally sick also and died tied to a tree behind their shack.

The Road

On this main road I observed many things as long as I lived in that house. I remember the man who stood outside on the step of a car, holding himself with his left arm to one of its doors. In his right hand he carried a megaphone to advertise the daily events of the day. He advertised the movie of the day, weddings and products on sale. He was known as Crazy Danny.

Like many other people, periodically I waited for a song book that was sponsored by a Mexican antacid, very popular in Vieques named "The Picot Grape Salt". That song book had many jokes, Mexican cartoons and the most popular Latin songs of the moment. The book was tossed from a car to all houses close to the road and at every store they left a few books for the customers of that store. This little book named *The Picot Grape Salt Songbook* became a topic of conversation. One could hear people talking about the jokes and the adventures of the short stories and cartoons, at barber shops, stores and on the streets and roads. I could never forget that little book because it was my favorite when I was young.

Almost every Sunday we saw Gene, the tobacco man, on his mare with two baskets on each side of the mare's belly. He distributed handmade cigars from his shop and also looked to buy some other things like eggs and other farm products to sell in his small store in town.

Catalina and Don Vale

In front of Catalina's house, by the side of the road, lived Don Vale. He was a very old, blind man who lived in a two-room little house. He was always accompanied by his dog, Jazmin. Catalina used to give him food and took care of the cleaning of the house. He was always clean and his house was in order. The few times that I visited him at his house I could smell the odors of the urine that he threw out of the side door. He was always barefoot, with his trousers tied at ankle level. He knew when bad weather was close. He stood in front of his house, smelled the air and said, "Look at the north, a storm is approaching! Look at the south, the birds are fleeing!"

As far as I can remember, Catalina lived with her son, Gilberto. Her other son, Jesus, also lived in her house, with his wife, Provi, his son, Lin, and his daughter, Lina. Lina always saved some apreens for me every time I visited them.

Catalina's farm was divided into two sections. One section, the one close to the beach, was dedicated to pastures, and the other section to sugarcane. When Catalina walked down her farm to check on the plantations and on her cattle, she lifted her dress up to the waist and stuck it all the way up to her panties to avoid the thistles to adhere to her cloth. We kids considered it fun to look at those white and wrinkled legs of hers. Catalina's farm was next to Dominga's farm. That is why we kids knew a lot about Catalina's way of living. Later on, Jesus moved to Monte Santo with his wife and children. After Catalina's death, Dominga took care of Don Vale. She had to hire people to clean up the house. Don Vale knew the way to Dominga's and every afternoon he took his cane, a metallic can with a wire handle on top, his dog Jazmin and walked down the pathway in order to get his hot meal. Dominga filled up the can with enough hot food for him and the dog. He walked all the way back on his own, using his cane and dog as guides, sat in the front door of his house and he and his dog enjoyed the only meal of the day. When he had finished, he walked to the drum of water on the southwest corner of the house, washed the can and the spoon, walked back to the house and hung them on a nail on the wall of the living room.

Our Evening Stories

In front of Don Vale's house there stood a big Haguey tree. All the male youngsters used to get together there every afternoon to talk about the adventures of the day and joke. Robert the Moor, Cruz, Berto, Masin Rash, Masin the trumpet, Rogelio, and my brother Angel made the group of teenage boys that got together under that tree. There were many arguments and fights among those youngsters. I remember the evening when my brother came running very fast, jumped into the balcony, got into my mother's room, came out to the balcony and yelled to the ones who were chasing him.

"Stop right there, you two, I've got a machete in my hand and will chop the head off of any one who gets close to me!"

My mother, who was sitting on the rocking chair, said to him, "Put that umbrella back. With that umbrella you are not going to chop anybody's head off, you might break it, and I've got no money to buy another."

My brother went back into his room, went to bed and didn't show up for the rest of the evening.

On the balcony, and under the dim light of the kerosene lamp, my mother amused us with songs, reading, and storytelling. I remember the stories about Garibaldi, that brave Italian warrior who also served in France's armed forces. She sung many songs dedicated to Garibaldi, describing his heroic adventures in all the battles. She told us pirates' legends of Black Beard, Red Beard and Blue Beard. The most terrible of all them was Black Beard. He had a castle on a remote island deep into the ocean. He used to kidnap girls to take to his castle. After raping them and forcing them to do the cleaning of his castle, he made them disappear. Once he kidnapped a girl, raped her, got drunk and went to sleep. He had told the girl that while cleaning the castle she should never try to enter the red room. When he was sound asleep, the girl took the key, opened the red room and fainted when she saw many corpses of girls hanging from the ceiling of that room and all the blood on the floor. When she got up Black Beard was still sleeping. She managed to flee from the castle on a rowing boat and came to civilization, to announce the situation. Nobody paid attention to her because in those days it was the strong who ruled. The fate of that girl is another story.

Another story that she used to read to us was the story of "Genoveve du Bravant". The novel was about a girl who had been abandoned to her own fate in the woods. She was left there by relatives that didn't want her to participate in an inheritance. The girl found a goat in the woods and with fruits that she could gather and the milk of the goat she managed to survive. After many years lost in the woods she found the way out to civilization.

My mother also read to us stories from the Bible. On rainy evenings, she did all that in her room while we were in bed until everybody was sound asleep.

Many steamboats and sailboats from other countries used the seaport of la Esperanza to bring merchandise. Some couldn't get close to the pier because it was too shallow, those were anchored between the keys. Smaller boats had to go and receive the products. Angel, my older brother, joined his group of friends and during the evenings they rowed to the proximity of those cargo boats. They looked for things that the sailors needed or wanted from ashore and got a few things in exchange. It was a businesslike transaction in between the boys and the sailors. The sailors had to do that because they were not allowed to come ashore for whatever reason. The boys never asked the sailors about their origin. All they wanted was some kind of business with them. One night my brother brought home some tasteless brown crackers in a box. They didn't taste like the ones we were used to, like the salty soda crackers. They were so tasteless that my mother said, "Let me brew some fresh coffee and put sugar in it, that is the only way that I am going to eat these."

Later in my life, I learned that those crackers were matzos.

Back to School

I loved the first days of school, everything was brand new; new clothes, shoes, notebooks, pencils and the books handed out to us were brand new too. I loved to open the books and smell them in between pages. From first grade I was sent to third grade because the second grade was like a repetition of first grade, and I knew how to read and write Spanish perfectly, and had also learned the arithmetic basics. By moving to third grade, I didn't need to go over those subjects. Now in third grade, I started my first English classes. That subject was the most important one because all textbooks of science and arithmetic were in English. On the north side of the school's main building, at noon and after lunch, the kids played baseball. I loved to watch them playing and listen to the arguments that were unavoidable for their out or safe decisions. Many of the games finished at the point when the arguing raised anger among the players. Close to the kids' playground, there was a line of pine trees and, at the back of the trees, lots of low dry plants. The ball was handmade with threads taken from any fabric. When the ball reached that area, it was a sure homer because it was difficult to remove it when entangled up in those plants.

On the eastern side of the school, there was a path that led to the neighborhoods of the Pearl and Dirty Goat. To the north and very close to the school lived Madam Durieux. She lived with about six children and worked at home, doing tailoring as a seamstress. She was seen close to that Singer sewing machine from morning through afternoon.

The intermediate school was located across the road to the north on top of a small hill. It had been named the Second Vocational Unit. In front, it had row of flamboyant trees. When these trees were in bloom, it produced such a beautiful color effect that many painters used it as an inspiration. It was surrounded by sugarcane fields belonging to Don Jovo, a wealthy farmer who lived to the west.

Zoilo Navarro

To the northeast of our house lived Don Zoilo, very close to the slope of Adon's hill. He lived in a house built with lumber, roofed and walled with palm tree leaves. There were two houses, a bigger one and the little one where Zoilo lived. He was a bald-headed, short black man who always walked around barefoot, with no shirts, his trousers tied up at ankle level and a straw hat where he kept his chewing tobacco. His trousers were tied up to the waist with dry fibers that he took from the leaves of banana trees. On very few occasions did he wear his Sundial leather boots. He only used them when going to town.

There was a rumor that said that he was the man who had the largest penis in this world. People said that he used to tie it close to his knees with fibers of banana trees in order to make it go unnoticed.

There was a time when a tall, bow-legged black woman called Maria Sulla decided to move in at Zoilo's. She was so bow-legged that people said, "Damn, she has a space between those legs that a dog fight can fit into."

When she moved in, she used the help of two kids. When the night was over, early in the morning the next day, she was seen walking down the pathway in a hurry. She was seen with all her things bundled up on her head.

"Why did you leave Zoilo so quickly?" people asked her.

"Because Zoilo is a selfish man, man, man, man," she answered.

She had the habit of repeating the last word of the sentence, about four times, in a strange accent.

But suspiciously, people didn't believe her and murmured, "Humm... humm."

Zoilo lived alone and, knowing the mercifulness of Dominga, joined Don Vale every afternoon to look for a fresh, home-cooked hot meal.

One afternoon, when Dominga called Zoilo for dinner, he stepped on the stairway and was bitten by Jackie. Jackie was Don Diaz's dog.

"Oh my goodness, I've been bitten by that devilish dog!" he yelled.

"What happened?" Dominga asked.

He yelled and fell down on the stairway. When Dominga saw the torn bleeding ankle of Zoilo, she put the dish down and, as fast as she could, looked for a rag, soaked it with kerosene and wrapped it around Zoilo's ankle. Don Zoilo was so hungry that in a short time he grabbed the dish and went under the mango trees to have his dinner.

"Oops, this really hurts," he said.

"Do you want to go to hospital now?" Don Diaz asked him.

"I believe that in a couple of days everything will come to normal. This is not the first time that I've been bitten by a dog," said Zoilo.

And it was true. Two weeks later, Zoilo was walking around with no bandages on his ankle.

Zoilo used to sleep in a hammock, in the middle of one of his shacks. He said that one night he saw a rat sliding down the rope of his hammock. The rat ran on top of Zoilo, from toes to head, across the hammock and disappeared. The following nights he felt the rat again and again. He got tired of this situation.

"I am going to get ready for this damn rat and get rid of it forever," he said.

One day he sat in the front door of his shack to file his machete and make it as sharp as a barber's razor blade.

"Now that damn rat is going to get it," he said.

That evening he tied up the ropes of his hammock as tight as he could. It was time to go to sleep. He jumped up into his hammock and put his machete across and on top of his chest to wait for the damn rat. He stood still and very watchful. He wanted to cut the damn rat into two pieces. He waited and waited for that dirty rat, looking at the rope with wide open eyes.

"The rat is there! Let me wait until it gets closer!"

He sat on the hammock, lifted his machete in the air, and with one movement... swosh! He swung his machete at the rat. At the same time he cut the rope and…

There went Zoilo, his machete and his hammock down to the floor! His machete flew in the air and got stuck on the wall of the shack.

A deep breath… another deep breath… and another.

"For devil's sake, I almost killed myself! How stupid of me!"

Zoilo got up from the entangled hammock, all confused, fatigued and sat on the front door to rest and think all over about his stupidity.

It was a clear night with a full moon in the middle of the sky. From the front door he could see the glittering silver-like ripples and waves of the sea in the distance, and the glittering waves of leaves of the sugarcane fields. It was a beautiful night. The sounds of the sea waves joined the sounds of the trees and bushes to create a celestial music. Such a pretty night that could very well have been the witness to the disgrace.

"How stupid of me," continued Zoilo, talking to himself. He was grateful to God that he didn't get hurt from that incident. At that moment he forgot all about the damned rat and didn't even care if it was dead or alive. He got up from the front door, untangled the hammock, fixed the rope, hung it up again and jumped over and went to sleep. One sure thing was that he never saw the rat again.

Ma Paco was a man who looked like Zoilo. One day Ma Paco went to El Canon place. This was the place in town where the prostitutes had their business. When Ma Paco got in, one of the girls approached him and said, "Oh, good evening, Zoilo, what can I do for you?"

"I am not Zoilo, I am Ma Paco," he said.

"Hey, Zoilo, would you like a shot of rum?" she asked.

"Look, I am telling you again that I am not Zoilo, I am Ma Paco and I don't drink, all I want is something else!" he yelled.

"Okay, Zoilo, I understand, but I don't see any available girl around," she said.

"Well, I've got all the time to wait, I'll sit around here until you tell me what to do," he insisted.

"Zoilo, you'd better go home and rest for the day and come back tomorrow," she said.

"Look, girl of the devils, I've got plenty of money to pay. I am not broke and I keep telling you that I am not Zoilo, I am Ma Paco! I am Ma Paco! I am Ma Paco!" he yelled and yelled again and again.

The fame of Zoilo's penis was such that all prostitutes were well aware of it and were suspicious of anybody who looked like him.

So Ma Paco had to leave the place without satisfying his desires.

"Zoilo, Zoilo, Zoilo!" Ma Paco repeated over and over again on his way back. "Next time I meet that fellow I'm going to hit him on the head and put him to sleep for some time."

To the east of his house, Zoilo had a big mango tree that produced what I considered the most delicious fruit of that variety. It was named apple mango.

Months later, a family of three people went to live in Zoilo's house. The name of the woman was Sofia. She moved in there with her brother, Cruz, and her daughter, Tacita. They moved into the bigger of the two houses, the one in the north side. They were not relatives of Zoilo, but they lived very respectfully with each other. People suspected that when Sofia was young she had probably been a cabaret woman of happy living, meaning by that, a prostitute. She was well shaped, with a nice looking face. Tacita, her daughter, was a teenage girl. She was always talking about her dreams. She wished she could be a cabaret dancer. She left for Chicago while she was in her teens. Months later, Sofia showed us pictures of Tacita wearing a tropical dancer's gown with lots of ostrich feathers and a hat with a bunch of flowers on her head.

"Tacita made it! Tacita made it! She made her dreams come true!"

That was the expression of every youngster in the region. We really liked her because she was a very nice and jolly girl.

Cruz was Sofia's brother. He was a fellow who liked to dress very neatly every day. He was a farm worker, but every afternoon, after a bath, he dressed in well-pressed pants and long-sleeved white shirt with a bow tie. He wore white shoes and a hat leaning to the side of his head and tried to impress the girls in the neighborhood. He didn't smoke or drink any alcoholic beverage.

After some time he married one of Martina's daughters and moved to the United States.

During those days some merchants came house to house, selling clothes, fabrics and many other household goods. They usually had a mare with big baskets full of things. It was a very efficient means of transporting goods over hills, bad roads and pathways. The regular merchant for this area was called Pomuceno. Don Manolo used his Ford wagon for this purpose, but he had to leave it on the road. This way his sales were not as good as Pomuceno's because the people had to walk all the way down to the main road.

Master Penzort

Some time ago, a sailboat approached the Esperanza pier. A group of people got out of the boat. Nobody knew where they came from. They were a family who came from some country, probably fleeing for political or whatever reasons. They bought a lot, not too far down the road from where we lived and very close to the old winch of La Hueca. They built a house with a basement, and in that basement the owner installed a laboratory. I never learned about his experiments, but I had the chance to get into his laboratory and sneak around with one of his sons. He had a library with many books and manuscripts and lots of written notes on his tables. Right in that laboratory he spent days and nights immersed in his experiments. The neighborhood knew him as Master Penzort.

He and his family carried out their own religious acts in a very private way. This was not normal in this region. People used to go to church and pray on Sundays, but they remained at home. For this reason they were named the Moors.

Every time they got out of their dwelling, people said, "There go the Moors."

The older son of Master Penzort, Roberto, became a good friend of Angel, my brother, and Leo, one of his younger sons, was a friend of mine.

My uncle Juan fell in love with one of the Penzort girls. Every time he found people talking, he was so obsessed that he stuck his nose in and asked, "That the Moors, what?"

His friends made fun of him and every time they met they greeted one another by saying, "That the Moors, what?"

The Draft

Now that the United States was committed to war in Europe the draft started. All men between the ages of twenty and forty-two had to go to Puerto Rico to get a physical examination to determine their eligibility for being drafted. Catalina's son, Berto, was drafted and sent to the Pacific to join General McArthur's forces in the war in Okinawa. Librada's son, Tony, was sent to a U.S. army camp in Texas. My brother, Angel, was sent as a military policeman to the islands of Trinidad and Aruba. Many others outside our neighborhood were sent to Europe to join the forces fighting there.

And We Moved Again

Uncle Alexander passed away. All my uncles got together and decided to let my mother take over his house to live in. We moved during the evening, as was customary in those days. My mother, my brother, Nestor, and I took over the task. Angel was in service down in the Caribbean islands. The house was old and not well conserved due to the advanced age of my uncle. He was one of my mother's oldest brothers and was born in the nineteenth century. The house had two bedrooms, a living room and of course the kitchen. The construction resembled Dominga's house, though on a smaller scale. The house wall to the north was a little deteriorated with some holes on the boards that we could see through. To get into that area there was a pathway whose entrance was in front and across the road from the grocery store of the Diaz-Velez. A few steps into the pathway, it turned to the left, went over a small hill, then turned right, and straight up until it reached Uncle Rafael's house. From there it turned left again to reach our house.

That was another step on our route to destiny.

There were two big rocks at the first turn to the left on that pathway, and between those rocks there was a big Haguey tree. This place was used by pedestrians, up and down the main road. The nice shade that the tree provided, together with a fresh breeze coming from the Caribbean Sea, was the perfect resting place for many pedestrians who wanted to escape the burning sun on those hot days.

The Tabaiba Worm

Close to the small hill going up the pathway, and to the entrance of Don Fele's lot, there was a tree that had many ugly-looking worms called Tabaiba. They were about six inches long, half an inch thick, with black, red and yellow stripes. They were all hairy and scary. It gave us the creeps to walk under that tree. Every time the wind blew and shook its branches, some of the worms fell to the ground. Coming back from school, we kids had to wait for the blowing wind to pause, and then taking turns, we ran to the other side as though fleeing from the devil. This way we avoided the possibility of having the worms fall on top of us.

Luis Bam Bam, the son of Amador, was the most fearful of all kids. For this reason Bert the Moron went ahead of us many times, grabbed one of those worms and hid behind a tree in the pathway. When Luis got close to him he suddenly got out and showed him a worm. Luis, with wide open eyes and trembling lips that showed how frightened he was, screamed and ran for his life. How disgusting those worms were!

The New Neighborhood

Our new home was a more comfortable place because, as we thought, we didn't have to move anymore. We thought that this was the end of our route. We had a house of our own, with enough land to raise animals and to grow plants, either garden vegetables, medicine plants, herbs, spices and fruits. We had about an acre and a half to use. We were surrounded by my uncles. Our house was right in the middle of a lot of about eight acres of land belonging to my grandmother, Felipa Monet. To the east lived Uncle Rafael, Uncle Cleo and Grandma. To the west lived Uncle Lolo. All my uncles raised chicken, pigs and goats, except Uncle Cleo who also raised some cattle. He used about four acres of land. From our house we could see the coastline from the cliffs of Pitirre to the seaport of La Esperanza. We had the hill of Don Fele to the south and that interrupted the view in that direction towards the Caribbean Sea. My grandmother had her little house by the pathway. She had a very tall sea grape tree in her yard. It was abnormal because sea grapes used to grow on sandy terrain on bushes by the beaches. This was probably an ancient bush that grew that tall with the passing years.

To the north, lived her sister Manen on a lot of about eight acres, close to the slope of Adon's hill. To the left side of Manen's house lived Nene Emerie and Fonso. Fonso was a First World War veteran. He told us of his adventures at war while fighting in Europe. He taught us how he aimed and fired a cannon in those days. He made his tales very interesting by showing us the military ways with peculiar movements of his body. He also talked about the strict discipline that they had to observe while in service. His wife Virginia was the seamstress of the neighborhood. She was sewing dresses all day long for many of the girls and women from our neighborhood and nearby places. She had a Singer sewing machine. She used the Aldens and the Sears catalog for the girls to select the fashion they preferred.

Fonso was a farm worker and a fisherman. He kept his fishing boat anchored at the Pass of the Boats. He sold his catch in the neighborhood. He and Don Guille made and repaired their fishing nets at a shack east of their homes and close to the sesame seeds plantation. The kids knew Fonso as Moroco. Fonso didn't like to be called by that name. Many times my grandma asked Bert the Moron and me to clean up her yard. Fonso lived on the northern side of Grandma's. After a few moments, when Bert and I started to do the cleaning, Bert started to yell at Fonso's house, "Moroco. Moroco, Moroco!"

Fonso opened the front door and we had to run and hide down the pathway.

"Who is putting names in there?" he asked.

He walked around the house, looking for whoever and, not finding anybody, walked back to his house again. That was repeated many times on the day until we finished the clean-up.

Very close to Andino's well, up the hill, lived Eduvigis with his wife, sons and daughters. Eduvigis was a short, rustic man. He had a pretty daughter by the name of Teresa. Berto, Catalina's son, fell in love with Teresa. He was so interested in her beauty that he took a chance in order to make sure that he was not going to lose her. So he walked all the way up to Eduvigis's house. When he reached the house he asked Eduvigis, "Sir, can I talk to you a minute?"

"Yes, son. What can I do for you?" asked Eduvigis.

"Well, I want you to know that I am in love with Teresa and would like to formalize an engagement, that is, I want to ask you for the hand of your daughter," Berto continued.

"Why do you want a hand for, why don't you take her complete?" responded Eduvigis.

"Look, sir, I want a formal engagement," Berto said.

"Do you really love her?" Eduvigis asked.

"Yes, with all my heart," Berto answered.

Eduvigis got up and yelled, "Teresa, come over here!"

Teresa opened the door and, knowing how rustic her father was, came out showing signs of her fear with wide open eyes and almost shaking.

"Do you love this man?" Eduvigis asked Teresa in a very loud voice.

"Yes, Dad, I love him," she answered.

"Well then, go for your things, pack up and get ready to leave with him right now," said Eduvigis.

"But, sir, all I want now is a permission to get engaged," Berto said.

"Damn it! If you love her you take her right now, why do you want to wait, you fool? Do you understand?" said Eduvigis.

"Yes, sir, but let me go home first in order to arrange things, and I will come back for her later on," said Berto.

Berto left the place and never came back. He was very young and not ready for marriage yet.

Years later, I heard that Teresa married a military person who took her to Japan. There, he got out of the service and continued working and living in Japan forever. She had an Oriental look, so for that reason she probably made it to Japan with no problems.

To the south of our house there was a fence between Don Fele's farm and ours. There was a line of Haguey trees. On one of those trees I built my tree house with some lumber that I found lying around our lot. I used this house to do my homework, to read, daydream and have a siesta. A fresh breeze coming from the sea made it a very fine location for my house. Close to the house there was a variety of breadfruit tree that produced many seeds. When one of those fruits fell down from the tree, I climbed down my tree, took the fruit, removed all the seeds and boiled them all in salt water to make them taste better.

I had a fireplace and a pot ready by my tree.

I always shared the boiled seeds with my family.

There was a valley in between our lot and Don Fele's. There, he had a sugarcane plantation. Across the valley there was a hill where he had his house. Every evening he played the saw. He had a saw that, when played with a violin's bow, sent into the air very melodious musical notes. He flooded the atmosphere with romantic melodies every evening. He also raised cattle and goats. I loved to go by his house because his wife Aurora made very delicious fried arepas. She made them very small compared to the regular ones that were about five inches in diameter. Her arepas were about one inch and a half. She always kept them on tray on top of the dining table. She always invited whoever passed by the house to come in and have some of her arepas. She was very proud of her cooking. Every time I walked by her house, I made some kind of noise in order to be heard by Aurora and be invited in.

The Spirits

Many strange things happened to me in the house that we had moved into.

The first incident happened a few days after we had moved in and while we had gone to sleep. My brother Nestor and I had a hammock each to sleep in in the living room. One night I heard a humming sound coming from underneath my hammock. When I looked down I saw a brilliant light illuminating a cut hand.

"What is that Nestor?" I asked my brother.

"What is what?" he said.

"That bright hand that is moving around my hammock!" I said.

"You must be nuts, I don't see anything," he said.

That thing kept moving around and around, faster and faster until it vanished.

From that moment on I shut up and said nothing else. I didn't want him to believe that I was crazy.

Something else happened to me another evening. I went to sleep and when I laid down I felt very cold air getting inside my body. It gave me the shivers. I moved around and around my hammock, but that thing kept getting deeper into my body until I fell asleep.

Some nights I used to hear a whistle that came from the roof. Then I saw something walking around the living room for a while until it disappeared. I heard my uncles saying that Uncle Alexander used to do that almost every evening. I didn't mention this to anybody because I was afraid of being taken for a nutty kid.

Another day I was walking by the east side of the house, when a strange force started to push me towards the barbed wire fence. I tried to move against that force but that thing was stronger than I was and tossed me against the wires. My legs and arms were wounded. I went to my mother to cure my wounds.

"How did that happened?" she asked.

"You wouldn't believe it, something strange pushed me against that fence," I answered.

"Stop talking nonsense, and tell me the truth, no strange things come just from the air. You should be more careful when walking around," she said.

I kept quiet and said nothing else while she was washing my wounds.

My mother's aunt, Manen, passed away. That night while all the neighborhood was at Manen's house watching her corpse in the coffin, I decided to go home, have some coffee and go to sleep. It was past midnight. I went into the kitchen. The kitchen had a window to the south where a pan of water was placed to wash the kitchen utensils. It had a door to the entrance of the house and a door to the yard, on the eastern side. I got into the kitchen and lit the fire. I put the coffee pot on the fire when all of a sudden the door to the east slammed shut. Immediately, I ran to see who had done that, but the door was closed tightly. I thought that somebody was playing games with me. I made sure that both doors and the window had been tightly closed. I leaned with my back to the window, waiting for some other doors to slam. To my surprise, the window that was shut on my back opened up and I was slammed on my back. *How could that happen?* I thought. *The window is still closed*. In an instant, all the doors and the window continued opening and closing for a few seconds. After that, everything was silent. Calmly, and in spite of being in a shivering state, I drank my coffee and went to sleep. I never mentioned this to anybody for the rest of my life for obvious reasons. Many other things happened to me, but that is another story.

Many years later in my life, I learned that Uncle Alexander hated my father to death and that was the reason why he wanted to separate Angel, my older brother, from my mother while she lived with my father. I was the only son who looked very much like my father. This meant that he took his revenge on me, against my father.

After Librada's son, Tony, was drafted into the U.S. army, and while he was on training, he visited my sister Alice in this house. Just before his overseas assignment, they got married. She received some allowance for being a dependant of Tony's. My mother also received the same amount of money for being a dependant of Angel's. With some of the money saved, they bought Gene Velez's house to use its lumber to build a bigger house on the same site. That was done. In the meantime, while the construction was in progress, we moved to Grandma's house.

After a year in service, both Angel and Tony had a one-month pass that they spent in our house before returning to service.

The Accident

During those days, my uncle Cleo was working for the U.S. navy on the construction of the magazines in Mosquito. One day at noon, we heard somebody screaming up on the hill of Andino. The whole neighborhood got out of their houses to check what was going on. Most of the men ran uphill to see who was screaming and why. They found Uncle Cleo laying on the ground with a bleeding and broken leg. They lifted him from the ground and carried him home. They put some boards on two sides of the leg and tied them with rags in order to put and keep the bones in place.

"What happened to you, why are you hurt?" some men asked.

"A steel beam fell on my leg and broke my bones," he answered.

"Who brought you here?" the men asked again.

"Nobody, I had to drag myself up and downhill from Mosquito, using that piece of wood," he said.

"That must have been painful. Why didn't anybody help you come over?" they said.

"You know how it is, nobody leaves work until they get their pay in the afternoon and I couldn't wait that long," he said.

There was no dispensary available. The U.S. navy was not responsible for accidents at work. If somebody died or got hurt because of an accident, the corpse was set aside until the afternoon. The workers managed to bring the body to that person's home. There was no ambulance service either from the navy or from the local government. There was a hospital, but no transportation available. To go to the hospital a person had to do it on his own, either on horseback or afoot. To move hurt people from the navy area, they mostly used a hammock tied to the ends of a long pole. One man at each end of the pole carried the corpse or the wounded.

The U.S. navy didn't keep a payroll record. They paid the

workers in cash in the afternoon for the hours worked during the day. If a worker left early he lost his pay for that day. That is why the workers didn't want to take care of their fellow workers when hurt during working hours. There wasn't even a first aid group to take care of them. Everyone worked at their own risk, with no guaranteed safety.

Public transportation became very scarce after the closing of this western area. Very few people remained to live close to the western area. There remained only a few farmers, and other families who at least had a horse to move from one place to another. The only public cars that served that area came in the morning. The cars brought the teachers from town to the school of Puerto Real. They didn't want to return to town with no passengers, so they drove around through the other boroughs to get some passengers. Two chauffeurs named Pablito and Manolo Brignoni were the ones who took care of that precarious situation. The place to get the cars back to the rural areas was located at a grocery store in the main street in town. That place was named Bolo's Place. The cars were available at noon. I remember a woman who wore lots of jewelry on her entire body. She used to sing all types of songs all the way to and from town. Her name was Tilita.

The Religious Instructions

I was in the fourth grade when I started to get religious instruction from Catholic priests. They came after school hours and took all the kids to the lunch room. There, we were instructed for the First Communion ceremony. The priests were either from Spain or from the United States. There was no church in our region. Catholic masses were offered at a conference room that belonged to the Vieques Chapter of AFL-CIO Labor Union, in the Lares sector of Puerto Real. This place was previously used as a school room when schools in the west were shut down. Just before the ceremony of the First Communion, we had to confess our sins to the priest in charge. On that day my brother Nestor developed a toothache. My mother had no medicine at hand and gave my brother some rum to hold in his mouth, so as to anesthetize it a little bit.

"Take this and hold it. Just before you get to the confessor, spit it out on the street," said my mother.

"Okay, Mom, I'll do that," said Nestor.

The moment approached and it was Nestor's turn for confession. He kneeled down at the confession booth and when he opened his mouth the priest smelled rum and asked, "Hey, son, do you drink rum?

"No, sir," Nestor answered.

"Look, son, you are here to confess and you start with a sin because you are lying. The smell of rum in your mouth is so strong that anybody can smell it, even a mile away," said the priest.

"No, what happened is that I had a toothache and my mother gave me some rum to hold in my mouth until just before confession," Nestor answered.

The priest was a Spaniard who liked to drink a lot and always had a long cigar in his lips. He looked suspiciously at my brother and said, "My son, you can drink, drink and drink, but please, never get drunk."

The Second World War is Over

This happened when I was in fourth grade. The news spread through the whole island.

"The war is over, the war is over!"

I saw people running back and forth, yelling, dancing and jumping. The whole island had been flooded with joy and happiness. People ran around from house to house spreading the news.

"Oh, how happy I am, my son is coming back home!" I heard and saw mothers say with tears in their eyes and full of joy. Many people said, "Great, the stupid rationing of goods will be over."

The rationing of goods was a terrible situation, especially for the substitute of lard. They distributed a synthetic grease as a substitute of lard which, when consumed, came out of the digestive system almost unnoticed, and without pain. That thing stained the cloth and it looked awful on the person's butt. This type of grease was not absorbed by the digestive system.

In school, when the news came in, the teachers let us go to the yard to celebrate the end of the war.

So all the kids jumped, danced and played around, having as much fun as they could have. Then they gave us permission to leave. That was an unforgettable event.

I passed on to the fifth grade. The teacher was a tall, skinny, black, bald-headed man whom people called Mr. Basa. He was named Mr. Basa because he played the bass in the municipal band of the town.

One day, while I was attending classes, Pablo, the student sitting behind me, using a rubber band as a slingshot, threw a piece of paper that hit Felicita in her ear. She sat in front of me. Quickly she turned around and slapped me in the face.

"What is going on in there?" asked Mr. Basa.

"This boy hit my ear with a slingshot," she said.

"I didn't do it, Pablo did it," I said.

"Oh yeah, come over here," the teacher said.

He came very furiously to my seat, grabbed my arm, pulled me out, hit me with his fist on my back, and dragged me out of the building. At the same time a whole bunch of bees came through the basement window. The bees stung Mr. Basa several times on his bald head.

"Come on, kid, get some water from the cistern and pour it on the ground. Hurry up!" he said.

I ran to the hallway, got a bucket of water and poured it in front of him.

"Come, kid, make some mud and put it on my head. Come, please help me!" he said.

Immediately, I did what he said and took my revenge. I rubbed and rubbed the mud very hard on his head.

He probably felt my vengeance and said, "Okay, that is enough, let's go back inside and forget all this."

The Second Vocational Unit

Sixth grade on to the ninth was offered at the school north of Barbosa. That school was known as the Second Vocational Unit. It was located on a hill surrounded by sugarcane fields. It had six classrooms, a lunchroom to the north side and the principal's office in the southwest corner. It was a reinforced concrete building, with a pretty architecture. It also had two cisterns on top of the building. They depended on water pumped from a little dam out to the east of the school. To the west, there was a huge water tank. It had a rectangular form and it was supposed to be a water reservoir taken from the dam. The pump was never used because it operated on electric power and this utility was not available in the region.

In the school yard, to the west, we had the volleyball court. We played almost every time we had a class break or during recess time. Mr. Ventura, the industrial arts professor, took the initiative to get a power generator and we installed it near his classroom at the eastern end of the school. When he started the generator, it made such a loud noise which was multiplied by the echo of the reinforced concrete walls of the building. That made such a terrible loud deafening sound that nobody could hear anybody when conversing in a normal way. We had to scream in order to be heard. Since this was the case, Mr. Ventura decided to make a hole in the ground, deep and wide enough to place the generator and do maintenance on it. That way the loud noise had to come down. After the generator was properly installed, the school activities improved. Now we could have parents-teachers night meetings, social activities and student activities. We also had volleyball practice and tournaments at night.

The Second World War veterans, taking advantage of the GI Bill approved by Congress, started to attend school. They went back to school to improve the education that they had left behind because of the precarious economic situation of the days prior to the war.

There, while in the sixth grade, I met Bonifacio, a veteran from the war in Germany. We noted that he had few fingers missing in his left hand. Our curiosity made us kids ask him, "What happened to you on that hand?"

"Oh, that happened in Germany," he said.

"How did it happen?" we asked.

"Well, it happened this way. Our company was moving in a patrol across a field in Germany. We found a railway and moved on it, looking for a group of German soldiers who were supposed to be in this area. All of a sudden we were ambushed by German soldiers who were hidden in the bushes around. Since we were in the open it was easier for them to shoot at us. We were an easy target. They shot at us with machine guns. Everybody went down and two corpses fell on me. I stood still on the ground, making the Germans believe that I was dead. After they made sure that they had killed everyone they came out of the bushes touching every one on the ground with their bayonets," he said.

"But how come you are alive?" we asked.

"Well, the two dead soldiers who fell on me saved my life. When the Germans touched everyone with their bayonets, they missed me because I was under them."

"But, how about your fingers?" we insisted.

"Oh well, it happened that when I fell down my hand was on top of a rail. I couldn't remove my hand from the rail, I didn't want the Germans to know that I was alive. When a train passed by, the wheels cut my three fingers off," he said.

"Ouchchch, we can imagine how painful it was!" we said.

"Well, I didn't feel much pain at that moment because it was winter time and the rails were cold. My hands were almost frozen, and I was so frightened that I didn't feel any pain at the beginning," he said.

"But, how did you get out of there?" we asked.

"I was freezing, when about four hours later the Red Cross came to recover the corpses. They were surprised when they saw me alive. I was the only survivor of that attack," he said.

"What an adventure, you must still be scared of that," we said.

"Not at all, those times have already passed away, all I want is to forget everything," he said.

After that we insisted that all the veterans in school tell us about their adventures while in service. They talked about battles, love adventures and all sorts of stories, probably true or just made up to entertain us.

Don Jovo

Don Jovo was the owner of almost all the farms around the school and to the west of it. He was always nattily dressed. He looked like a British Lord. He wore shiny, knee-high leather boots. His khaki shirt and pants were well pressed and he wore a British hard hat, one of those that you saw people wearing during safaris. He moved around his farms on a fine horse over a very expensive saddle and bridle. His accent was rather peculiar. He lived in a mansion that he had built on top of a hill, not too far from the schools. It was located to the west of the schools. The mansion had a rectangular form, made with reinforced concrete walls and roofed with corrugated metal sheets. It was painted light yellow on the walls and bright red on the roof. He was the only farmer in this region who had a fleet of cargo trucks. He rented his trucks to farmers to transport sugarcane bales to La Central, to the piers, to the winches and rented them also to businessmen for general transportation of merchandise. He owned a great extension of land in the central part of the island. He had a mistress in almost every sector of the neighborhoods that he owned.

Once, he lost his wallet in a sugarcane field that he was checking out. The humble and honest man who found it went to his mansion to return it.

"Excuse me, sir, I found something that belongs to you and I came in all the way to return it," the man said.

"Us, us, hell, hell what is it?" asked Don Jovo in his peculiar accent.

"Well, sir, it is a wallet that has your name on it, so I suppose it belongs to you," the man said.

"Us, us, hell, hell, where did you find it?" asked Don Jovo.

"I found it on the pathway near the Martinez house, a little bit down the hill," said the man.

"Us, us, hell, hell, and how much money is in it?" asked Don

Jovo.

"I don't know, I wouldn't never dare look into other people's belongings, but if you are generous enough and give something to me, I would really appreciate it," said the man.

"Us, us, hell, hell I would really like to give something to you," said Don Jovo.

"I would be very grateful to you, sir," the man said.

"Us, us, hell, hell, do you know what you deserve? You deserve a beating and I would beat the hell out of you for being such a fool. This wallet has four hundred dollars in it, and if I had found a wallet with that kind of money I would never have given it to nobody. Us, us, hell, hell get out of my sight and don't show up around anymore, I wouldn't like to see you anymore in my life. Get out, you fool!"

All the trucks that Don Jovo owned looked very deteriorated. This was due to the hard work that they were submitted to and the poor road conditions on the island.

The Navy's Pullout

The Second World War was over. The U.S. navy started to withdraw from Vieques. The magazines were emptied and all military equipment was removed from the island. The area was no longer needed because the threat to peace had ended. Both the Japanese and the Nazis had surrendered to the allied forces. That meant a lot of happiness to us, the residents of the western portion close to the navy area. Now we could go back to the lagoon, to the hills of Ventana, to the remains of Playa Grande, to the beaches of Mosquito, to Playa Vieja and to the fishing areas on the western beaches. Now we could go hunting wild pigs and goats. We could go for fruits and for firewood, so much needed in our homes. Now we could go hunting crabs on the mangroves of the lagoon and collect coconuts in the forests around the lagoon.

At the first opportunity, my uncles went fishing to Salinas on the eastern side. They spent few days there and brought enough fish and lobsters for their family and relatives.

Luis Bam Bam, Bert the Moron and I got together to take a trip into the western area to search for whatever we might need in the future. We got up early before dawn one morning and took off through the hills of Andino, went across the navy's barbed wire fence and continued down to the Playita area. We walked to El Sapo, the place where I was born. There, we found the remains of the houses all crushed down and lots of metal sheets all corroded by time and humidity, as well as lumber all eaten up by termites and deteriorated with time and smashed down when the navy bulldozers destroyed them. My former house was there, lying in pieces on the ground.

After looking at that sad picture we walked down to La Central. I first went to see my father's place and the pieces of lumber were all over the place. It was difficult to distinguish anything. The machine shop was not there but the concrete floor remained almost untouched. The stone walls were there and the remains of La Central. We immediately ran into the locomotives parking area. What a surprise! The eight locomotives were right there! They were all covered up with grass and vines and dust. Luis ran around looking for No. 8. It was his father's machine. When he found it we immediately started to remove all the grass and vines that covered the machine. He sat on the driver's stool and pretended to be his father.

"Okay, let's move! Bam, bam, bam, bam." That was fun and happiness for us. We walked around the other machines, looking all over for whatever we could find to take as a souvenir. The smell of molasses was there. I was told that the smell of molasses would stay there for years and years. We looked down south to the Street of Fire. The place was full of bushes, trees and grass. The houses were all torn down, lying around. It seemed as if a hurricane had passed by and destroyed everything on its path. We continued looking all over La Central until we decided to walk down to the ancient well. There it was, full of leaves and a rare smell of something rotten. The water was dirty and around the well there was lots of grass and a muddy ground. The pump had disappeared.

It was late in the morning, but we had all day to continue our search. So we decided to go southwest to Playa Vieja.

"Hey, let's go to Playa Vieja and have some coconut water," said Luis.

"That is a great idea," said Bert.

"Why don't we cut a branch of a tree and make a spear? There must be lots of lobsters hidden in the rocks and the corals," I said.

"You are right, I brought some matches and we can roast them right underneath those magnificent palm trees," said Luis.

That we did. When we reached the place we stepped on the rocks on the beach and could see lobsters and fishes in abundance. We got confused at this time because we didn't expect to find so many fishes swimming around. Now we had to decide, either to catch fishes or lobsters. We decided for lobsters. Using the spears we caught four. Luis climbed up the green coconut palm tree and, using his hunting knife, cut down a whole bunch of coconuts. We made a fireplace with loose rocks and lit the fire. We placed the lobsters on top of the red hot rocks. We used as dishes the empty shell of dry coconuts that we found laying around. After our lunch, we took a little rest, lying on the sands of that beautiful beach.

We walked back but, instead of going back the same way, we walked east down to the south side of the lagoon. The wooden bridge across the mouth of the lagoon had disappeared. We had to go down the mouth in order to get to the other side of it.

When we got back to our homes we faced lots of questions from everybody around.

"How about this, how about that?"

They wanted to know every detail of the condition of those areas. People were hoping to return in a short period of time. They expected to see the town of Playa Grande rebuilt, as well as Mosquito and La Palma.

"The war is over. No more war threats in sight. Now we can recover the land. Our relatives can come back to restart a new way of life," people thought and talked about it. Everybody was happy and joyful. "This is great," many people shouted.

After that great adventure, Luis, Bert and I made plans for the future. At weekends we would get up as early as four o'clock in the morning to start our way, either to fish, to look for firewood in the lagoon, or to hunt wild pigs or goats.

In order to hunt wild pigs, we put some food underneath a tree that had a straight horizontal branch. We climbed up to that branch and waited. We made a lace on a rope and waited for the hungry animal. When the animal started to eat, we let the rope go down very slowly for the animal to get used to it. Then, very carefully, we tried to put it around his neck. When around its neck, we immediately pulled up the rope and hung the animal to the branch. We climbed down the tree, put the pig in a sack, tied both ends of the sack to a pole and carried it back home.

The goats were more difficult to catch. We had to hide in the bushes or grass and wait for them to approach us. Then we tried to lace them with a cowboy lace on the rope.

Fishing in the lagoon's mouth was an easier job. We sat on the rock barrier in the mouth of the lagoon. There we waited for the high tide in the evening. The high tide moved lots of salt water fish into the lagoon and we took advantage of that. At the moment when the tide was moving down we placed a net across the mouth of the lagoon, very close to it. Then we went to sleep right there on the eastern side of the mouth, on the sands of the beach, until the next day.

One night, while we were trying to sleep, I heard a strong humming sound coming from the western side across the mouth. I got up, went across the mouth towards the forest of palm trees in there. I noticed that the white sands in there had turned black. Through the darkness of the night, I looked very closely and saw thousands of female crabs on their way to the beach. They had their bellies full of eggs. As they reached the breaking waves on the beach, they stood still until their eggs were washed away. After their bellies were washed out, they returned to their caves by the thousands. That was a rare and spectacular show of nature.

We got up early in the morning, looked into our net and found lots of trapped fishes. Because of the low tide, they tried to go back to the sea. We got our sacks and filled them up with all the fish we could carry on our backs.

We used to go to the hills of Ventana to look for fruits. There we got avocados, limes, guavas and many other varieties of tropical fruits.

The Sugar Industry Came to an End

After the sugar mill was shut down, sugarcane was transported to Puerto Rico on barges, using the sea port of La Esperanza. I heard that the sugar mill was disassembled and moved to the state of Florida. They kept the same name of Playa Grande. During these years the government established a subsidy to compensate the farmers who grew sugarcane on their farms. This way many farmers who had abandoned the sugarcane started to plant it all over. The Puerto Rico Agricultural Company took advantage of this period of time and planted sugarcane on all the land available to them and also on U.S. navy land, to the southwest of the island. They also used all the land available from the Land Authority of Puerto Rico. The sugarcane bales were then transported to the winch north of Sun Bay. They were weighed, taken to the winch that lifted them up and placed in the wagons of the last locomotive available. This locomotive moved its train of loaded wagons to the pier in order to load the barges.

We kids loved to watch all this.

This didn't last too long because this whole process was probably too expensive. At this stage the sugarcane industry came to an end. Now, extreme poverty had reached the island. The loss of the sugar mill with all the direct and indirect jobs caused an economic disaster on the island. Many people started to move out of the island looking for a better way of life. They moved to the United States, to the U.S. Virgin Islands and to Puerto Rico. By the end of the decade of the forties the population of the island was near twenty thousand. Now approaching the fifties the population was reduced to about four thousand. The spinal cord of our economy had vanished forever. Our income now had to depend on the sale of animals, some farming and the very few government jobs.

Due to the lack of sugarcane, our soil started to dry out. The sugarcane straw was a means for trapping the humidity from the air, thus producing many small brooks around the island. By the time I was in first grade I was told that there were forty-eight brooks of fresh water on the island. By that time I could see many water pumps that operated with windmills. Windmills covered the whole coastline of the island. The island dried out and the windmills vanished. We, the people living on the west end, used the water from Andino's well. The water to that well came from three underground veins of water. It was real fresh, pure spring water. Laboratory tests carried out at the University of Puerto Rico proved that it was one of the purest waters on this planet. The well was protected by a round wall made with rocks. The veins of water were in the middle of it. The wall was about six feet deep and about nine feet wide. The people in the neighborhood used to clean it up from fallen leaves and even grown grass on the rock wall, every other month. There was a tree whose branches covered the entire top of the well with its shade. There was a fence around the well to protect it from animals and from contaminants. Right down, following the water current they build a trough for the animals. It was like a long channel that we kids used as a swimming pool in the afternoon. Many times after school hours, and after we got tired of playing around, we took off for a swim on the trough.

The water in town was taken from three wells located north of La Esperanza, to the right of the road going down from the Mine. This water was pumped to a cistern on top of a hill close to Martineau and then pumped down to town. That water was purified with chlorine and many times it tasted salty. It had to be ice cold to withstand that taste. That was one of the reasons for the high incidence of high blood pressure cases on the island.

Guateen's Sweetheart

My brother Guateen was not even a teenager when he got his first girlfriend. Let's say that he was around twelve years old. The girl lived down the road, close to La Hueca's brook and not too far from the Penzort family. Her father was the barber of the neighborhood and had his barber shop across the road from his house, almost underneath a big Haguey tree. They used to date late in the evening in her house. Guateen had a wooden box hidden in the bushes next to the house on the northern side, close to a trough. He used to go there at about nine o'clock during the evenings when everybody in the house had gone to bed. He would take the hidden wooden box, place it on the ground in front of his sweetheart's window. Then he would jump over the box and knock on the window several times with a code. She would get up from bed, stand by the window inside her room, and kiss and caress and do whatever they wanted to do until it was time to get out of there. Once, on a Friday evening, I went to my brother's house because Don Diaz had asked me to help him on his farm on Saturday. While I was in bed Guateen came to me and said, "Hey, Nello, get up and come with me to Lydia's house."

"Forget it, it is nine o'clock and nobody is going to take me out of bed. The night is too dark and cloudy. It might rain and we are going to get soaked and wet. Let's do it tomorrow," I told him.

Guateen took off, reached the trough, took off his shoes and put them on top of the concrete wall of the trough. He then looked for the wooden box, placed it as usual in front of the window and knocked several times as agreed. The girl didn't show up. He thought that she was sound asleep and decided to knock on the window once more. During those days it was customary to leave the windows open all night. In order to keep the mosquitoes away they put a mosquito net on top of the beds. Noticing that the girl didn't respond, he jumped on the window and into the bed of his girl. He got all tangled up in the mosquito net.

A scream was heard on that silent night.

"For all devils in this world, what the hell is this? What kind of an animal has fallen on top of me?" said Brigido, screaming.

When my brother realized that a man was in the bed instead of his girl, he hurriedly jumped out of the window and ran out through the pathway north of the house. The dog followed him barking and barking.

Everybody in the house got up with a lit kerosene lantern and ran to the room to see what was going on.

"What happened, what is wrong in here?" they asked.

"An animal got through the window, jumped over me, broke the mosquito net, jumped out again and ran in that direction. Listen to the barking dog, it is chasing that animal right now! Oh boy, how scared I was. It gave me the shivers!" said Brigido.

Guateen continued running, as though being chased by the devil, passing through barbed wire fences, a pathway up and a pathway down, trying to get rid of that damn dog. He finally made it home.

"Nello, get up!" he said.

When I looked at him, his shirt and pants were torn, he wore no shoes, and was sweating all over.

"What the hell happened to you? You look awful all over!" I said.

"Let's go outdoors and I'll tell you," he said.

"Tell me," I said.

We walked out and sat on the stairway by the kitchen. He told me the whole incident, with all the details.

"Lydia wasn't in her room. A man was sleeping in her bed and I fell on top of him. He screamed like an old lady. I had to run fast because that stupid dog followed me all the way. Please come with me to look for my shoes. I left them by the trough," he said.

"How are we going to pass by the house? The dog must be waiting there to chase us again," I said.

"Don't worry, I know another way to get there unnoticed," he said.

That we did. We walked all the way east and by the entrance to the Riveras' farm, we took the way up and then westward until we reached the trough. What had happened was that Brigido had an argument with his wife that day and asked Lydia's father for a room to spend the night in until everything calmed down at his home. He would return home early in the morning the following day.

The next morning the news spread all over the neighborhood.

"Do you know that an animal jumped over Brigido last night?"

"How could that happen? There are no wild animals in Vieques."

"He said that it looked like a monkey or something similar."

"Or it could have been one of those small dogs that you see around looking for food."

"Did he take a good look at it?"

"No, he said that he got so scared and it was so dark that he closed his eyes at that moment."

"I have my suspicions. It could have been one of those secret experiments of Master Penzort. His laboratory is not too far across the road."

People kept talking and talking for weeks about that strange incident. I knew the answer and so did Lydia, but we had to keep our mouths shut to avoid a beating from her father.

The Pirates' Treasures

The elderly people in Vieques relate stories and legends of pirates' treasures buried in places around the island. One of those places is the Doradilla Cavern on the highest hill of Ventana. The story goes that the pirates and other people liked to hide their fortunes in that cave. The reason was that the cave was very dark and every source of light taken in there was turned off by some strange force or ghost. That made it very difficult for anyone to find any hidden treasure.

They also say that there are many treasures buried in the beaches around the island. They say that a pirate used to take his treasure chest on a row boat to the beach, using two sailors to help him out. He asked the sailors to dig a deep hole in the sand. When the hole was very deep he killed the two sailors and kicked the chest into the hole. He buried the chest and the two sailors in the same hole. That way nobody could find the place where he had buried his treasure. When he returned to his ship he was asked, "What happened to our buddies?"

Right at this moment the pirate made up a story.

"I had to run for my life, your buddies met some native girls, robbed my chest, tried to kill me and disappeared into the island. I had to row back in a hurry to avoid being killed," he said.

There is a general belief that centuries have passed and many treasures are still lying somewhere around in the sandy beaches of Vieques. Legends are heard saying that the spirits of the murdered sailors are giving them away. They show up in somebody's midnight dream, tell the person the exact location of the buried treasure and give specific instructions on how to get it out, and the specific time at night, which is usually midnight. If the person does not follow the instructions as given he will never find the treasure. The most common instruction is to take it all or leave it all, which means that the selected person has to take the whole treasure home or otherwise he would never be able to find it again. If someone takes some of the treasure and does not return it by not taking it all, a curse falls on that person that will make his life miserable for the rest of his life. It happened once to a man called Juan Carmona. He was visited by a spirit who told him about a treasure. He went after the treasure, found it, took some gold coins, spent them, but didn't go back for the rest. His eyes popped out forever and he could never put them back in place.

Back to the West Side

The pull-back of the navy made our life a lot better. Our resources were expanded. Almost every Saturday we took off to the lagoon area to look for coconuts, to catch crabs, to look for firewood and whatever the lagoon could give us. For the first time I saw the Cayul tree. This tree bore a fruit that produced a very strong narcotic effect. I had heard people talking about it but had never been close to it. It was located on the northeastern side of the lagoon, close to uncle Sico's farm. The fruits were yellow, the size of an apple, with a soft pulp. They fell on the ground and when the vapors were smelled they produced a spell of dizziness in the animals. Being curious, I stepped underneath the tree and when I breathed in I almost fell down. I had to run out quickly for fresh air to avoid getting dizzy and to avoid falling down.

Other people took advantage of the navy's leftovers. The magazines were left open, with lots of lumber inside. All ammunition was removed from the area, making it very safe for people to get in. Looting of the area began. Many people built their houses with the lumber left behind in the magazines.

One person who took advantage of the situation was Vergè. This man removed all the old iron and steel parts left around to be sold to an iron processing plant in Puerto Rico. He transported them to San Juan in sailboats. He removed all rails from the rail tracks, dismantled the eight locomotives of La Central, took whatever steel or iron part was left in the sugar mill and its surroundings. He also removed many steel beams from the magazines. In other words, he cleaned up the whole area from old and rusty metal parts lying around.

In the beginning, when the navy pulled out, they left a commander in charge of the area. His name was Gordon Littlefield. He married a girl of British descent named Luisa Simmons. He was in charge of giving permits to people to remove things from the area and to groups picnicking on the beaches in the west, especially at Mosquito, Punta Arenas and Playa Vieja.

After he got out of the service, nobody was assigned by the navy to replace him. He continued living in Vieques. He opened a dancing and restaurant place in Monte Santo. The place was near the beach, by a ridge where the eastern coastline of the island of Puerto Rico was visible. He also had a bar in town, close to the seaport. Luisa had a catering service for activities on the island.

During those days, crab catching in the lagoon's mangroves was very popular. Being untouched for about five years gave these crustaceans the opportunity to multiply without being disturbed. Littlefield loved crab meat. Don Diaz and he were very good friends. Don Diaz needed pastures for his cattle from that area mostly in the dry seasons and Littlefield allowed him to take whatever he needed. On many occasions Littlefield came to our neighborhood looking for youngsters to help him catch crabs in the lagoon. He was not frightened of being bitten by the crabs. He stuck his hands deep into the caves and pulled them out with his bare hands.

The Ferry Boats to Fajardo

Don Diaz took advantage of those crab catches, and saved some for his relatives on the island of Puerto Rico. He made a few cages to put in about two dozen crabs in each one. He transported them on the ferry boat to Fajardo. There were no piers for passengers in that seaport. In order to reach the ferry there was a small rowing boat that took the passengers from a little pier by the beach. The same thing happened in Fajardo. So Don Diaz had to pay extra to move his cages from the beach to the ferry. He also transported chickens in cages. There never occurred an accident in the course of these movements. But during rainy days the situation was terrible and very uncomfortable for moving in and out of the boats, due to the distance from the ferry to the beach. The trip on the open sea was a torture. The smell of diesel, mixed with the smell of Jumasos, and later with the smell of vomiting, made this a terrible experience. At the end of the trip you didn't know whether you wanted to die or just vanish from the face of the earth. You had to have a stomach made of steel to resist the movement from side to side, front to back, and all the repugnant smells. The trip usually took about two hours in good weather. People always missed the olden days when a trip from Punta Arenas to Naguabo took only half an hour on a sailboat.

This seaport was the only one available for passengers. It was also used for moving light goods to and from Puerto Rico. The merchandise came in sailboats that were loaded from row boats, the same as passengers. They were loaded and unloaded manually by port workers. For the heavier merchandise they used the pier in the seaport of La Esperanza, to the south. That was a big pier with winches to lift heavy loads. Later on, a much needed pier was built in town to allow the sail and motorized boats to come to a secure place with their merchandise. Now, instead of anchoring out in the sea they could be tied to the pier, making it safer to load and unload their goods and passengers. The animals like cows, goats and pigs could be transported out without the risk of losing them at sea.

The Pathway

My brother Nestor had graduated from ninth grade and moved to Monte Santo in order to be close to the Vieques High School. He lived in Nini's house, a friend of my mother's. He allowed Nestor to stay in his house until graduation from the twelfth grade. It was too far to walk back and forth every day of the week, from home to town. He went there on Sunday afternoons and returned home on Friday evenings. Before Nestor went to high school he was in charge of getting half a gallon of milk from Don Diaz. He used to walk very early in the morning all the way down the pathway. When Nestor went to school, it was my turn to go get the milk. I saw some kids from our neighborhood taking the same trip for the same purpose. Some went to Bartolo's farm and some to Don Diaz's. The older daughter of Fonso used to go to Bartolo's for the morning milk. One morning, I noticed that when she passed by my side, she stopped, winked her eyes, smiled and continued walking home. I told that to one of my schoolmates.

"That girl is making fun of me," I said.

"How come, isn't she your neighbor?" he asked.

"Yes, but I see something strange in her eyes when she looks at me, when we walk down the pathway," I said.

"Are you a stupid ignorant? Don't you know that she wants something from you?" he said.

I was so young, about ten years of age, that I never thought before about anything to do with sex.

"What do you mean by something?" I asked.

"Oh, come on, she wants to be kissed, to be held tight and things like that," he told me.

I followed my friend's instructions. One day I saw her coming my way. When she stopped, I developed some courage and held her tight to my body. I walked back a little and looked at her. She was smiling, showing some satisfaction. After that, we continued on our way. Not a single word was said. After that day, I thought about it over and over again. The more I thought about it, the more scared I got. Afterwards, being so scared, I didn't want to meet that girl again. So I waited for her to pass me by while I was hidden behind the Higuera tree on the pathway.

Once I found a napkin with some coins in it.

"Mom, look what I found," I said.

"Where did you get that money from?" she asked.

"I found it by the Higuera tree," I answered.

"Okay, go back to the Higuera tree and put it back where you found it. This way whoever lost it will find it easily," my mother advised me.

I followed my mother's advice and did exactly what she told me to do.

Games, Sports

Our life continued in this neighborhood in the normal way. I was already a grown-up child and was able to participate in almost all the games and sports with the other boys. On afternoons and during weekends we had many games to choose from. We could play baseball, the marbles, the tops, beeyard, the wheel and the garapeen, fly kites go down the beach with our home-made tiny vessels, or slingshot hunting of birds.

We played baseball in a place down the slope, north of the Mounted Rock and west of Uncle Lolo's house. It was the only place available close to our houses. We made this place suitable for playing baseball, though it had a rock behind second base. This rock caused much confusion every time the ball hit it. We couldn't figure out what direction the ball was going to take. We named this park the Uphill Park. From home to first base we ran on a level terrain; from first to second we had to run uphill; from second to third on level terrain and from third to home we ran downhill. We made our own bats with wood from cut branches of trees. We formed them with our hunting knives and sanded them to make them smooth. The gloves were made with pieces of sailcloth that we found near the places where they built the sailboats. Those were sewed on the Singer sewing machines that most women had in their homes.

Wheel and garapeen races were held on the main road. We had the starting and finish line in front of Bartolo's store. We went running west to Andino's bridge and back to Bartolo's. Or we went east to Jose's barber shop and back to the same place.

The beeyard game was the one that I liked the most. This game needed a lot of space in order to play it. Since the traffic on the main road was very rare, we selected the area on the road in front of Gene Velez's store to start the game. There we drew the circle and tossed a coin to select the first hitter. Many times the bee used to fly out to a nearby farm. The hitter continued hitting it until somebody could catch it in the air. Adalberto, the son of Gabriel Garambois, liked to play this game for a specific reason. He liked to chase Luis with a gongolie. Luis detested those insects. Every time we had to follow Luis in a farm, Adalberto put a gongolie on a cut piece of a branch and chased Luis all over. But Luis knew that Adalberto was afraid of lizards. At the very first chance during the chase, Luis grabbed a lizard hid behind a tree and waited for Adalberto. Adalberto looked around and suddenly Luis jumped over him with the lizard. The chase was reversed. And that went on and on, taking turns until late in the afternoon, when we were all exhausted. That was the end of the beeyard game, with no winners. We could only play a complete game when Adalberto didn't show up.

We also played marbles in a variety of ways. We played the three holes, the circle on the ground and the one that is played on straight ground.

The saramba game was the most dangerous of games. The saramba was a top that we made out of hard wood taken from the guava plant trunk. This top was about four inches in diameter. We put a one-quarter-inch thick nail, sticking out about an inch and a half and sharpened it to make it pointed. With this saramba we tried to split into half the other tops lying on the ground. We liked to toss it very fast. If it bounced back it could hurt any one of the players. Since we often played this game barefooted, our parents chased us out of it.

The most beautiful of games were the boat regattas. We made our own sailboats. We saved all the lead that covered the pack of cigarettes to be melted and used as ballast. We made the boat with soft wood from a tree called Almacigo. The bark or the branches of the tree were also used as medicine. After we cut part of the trunk, we managed to make the boat about eighteen inches long in a symmetric form. We sanded it very carefully and determined the amount of masts that we could put to make it faster while pushed by the wind while on the sea. We made the holes on the side of the boat with a red hot nail. These holes were necessary to hold the cords of the masts. We painted it either blue and white, green and white or red and white. The darker color was always on the bottom part, the one that was in contact with the water. We asked Virginia, the seamstress, for leftover rags in order to make the sails. The process took a long time. All the kids got together to determine the date of the regatta. When everybody was ready, we took off for the Pass of the Boats. We followed the routes of our boats very closely by swimming alongside them. But sometimes we were surprised by a big wave and the boat took off in another direction. This way we lost many of them. We sat on the sands on the beach to watch them disappear from our sight, deep into the sea.

We also made our own toy cars and trucks. We made them using whatever piece of lumber we could find in the neighborhood. The wheels were made out of empty cans of juice or sausages. We flattened the bigger can and fitted the small top of the can on it. Then we put a nail across the middle to serve as an axle. In order to guide the cars we used a long pole. The pole's front tip was placed on top of the cabin. At the other end of the pole we nailed a piece of wood, which served as a crossbar for the driver to guide the truck. The piece of wood had strings tied to it and to the front wheels. This way we could guide the cars in whatever direction we wanted them to go.

At least one Saturday of every month, we had an adventure in the sea. We took a big tractor tube and took off to La Esperanza. The tube was taken from one of those tractors that had two small tires in the front and two big tires on the rear. We took the tube from one of the rear tires. We put air into the tube by blowing it in with our mouths. We put a piece of corn cob to hold the air in. At the very tip of La Esperanza pier we put the tube in the water and all of us jumped into the water. We swam into the sea in between the two keys, turned westwards, and continued swimming alongside the tube, about a mile off the coast. The tube was used to rest on, on our way bound to the west. My brother Guateen used to take the cob off the tube and would toss it as far as he could into the water. Lolo, one of my cousins, got scared and started blowing air in to replace the lost air. Others took off swimming after the cob to bring it back. This was repeated many times until we were pushed by the waves to the beach of Playa Grande, just west of the mouth of the lagoon. That was about a four-mile swim.

Kite flying on the hills of Andino was one of our favorites. The wind blows constantly in this region, making it very comfortable for this event.

Slingshot hunting of birds was another sport that we liked a lot. We always selected the big birds that we could roast and eat.

We liked to tame young horses. That was like a sport to us. We took the young horses to the Pass of the Boats. There, we pulled the horse to go deep into the water. In that instant we mounted the horse. The horse was trapped by the water pressure and could hardly move. We made it walk around inside the water for as long as it was needed. Then, we made it walk to the sands of the beach to see if it was already tamed. This way we avoided being kicked or bitten while mounting them. It was a safe method to tame horses.

Gabriel's Goat

Gabriel Garambois and Gene Velez had been good friends ever since they were kids. Even at this age they used to get together every afternoon to chat, tell jokes and to have a general conversation as usual. Gabriel lived not too far east from us.

One of those days Gene went to Gabriel's home for a visit. After a long conversation on that evening they bid each other goodbye and Gene went back home. He noticed that on the side of the road there was a little goat tied to the fence on Gabriel's side. He got close to the goat, took it by the rope and took it home. There, he tied it to the fence on the southern side of the house, close to the cane field.

The following day Gabriel came to Gene's house. "Good afternoon," said Gabriel.

"Good afternoon, why are you here so early?" asked Gene.

"My friend, many strange things are happening in this world nowadays," said Gabriel.

"What happened?" asked Gene.

"Well, I had a goat tied to a fence at the back of my house and when I got up this morning it had vanished from the face of the earth," said Gabriel.

"Don't tell me, my friend, I can't believe such a thing could happen in this neighborhood," said Gene.

"I really don't know how it happened, the goat couldn't have escaped or gotten loose because I made sure that the knot I made on the rope was very tight," said Gabriel.

"Could anyone have stolen it?" asked Gene.

"That is a possibility," said Gabriel.

In the meantime, while Gabriel and Gene were talking the goat bleated several times. Without moving from his seat, Gabriel figured out the direction of the bleats. It was already dark in the evening and Gabriel decided to go home.

He pretended that he had gone, but instead he hid behind a

tree next to Gene's house. When the lights went off Gabriel went to the rear of the house and took his goat back home.

The following day Gene visited Gabriel.

"Good evening, my friend," said Gene.

"Good evening," answered Gabriel.

"Do you know something?" asked Gene.

"Oh no, you tell me," said Gabriel.

"The same thing that happened to you the other night happened to me last night. I had a goat that disappeared from my house," said Gene.

"Is that true, my friend?" asked Gabriel.

"Like I tell you. I woke up early in the morning and the goat had disappeared," said Gene.

"Well, from now on we must be very careful, and watch our animals very closely. Where are we going to go if things continue this way? Both of us lost our goats. Now, what is next?" said Gabriel.

After this Gene said goodbye to Gabriel, walked up the road and hid in the bushes. He had to wait for the lights to go off in Gabriel's house and then figure out where Gabriel had tied the goat. He walked around and found it. He started to untie the rope when, suddenly, Gabriel showed up with a machete in his hand lifted in the air, ready to cut whatever. Gene became so scared that he fell down, looking with frightened eyes at Gabriel.

"What are you going to do, my friend?" asked Gene.

"This has to come to an end," said Gabriel.

"You are not going to kill me for a simple thing?" said Gene.

"This came to the very end," said Gabriel and at the same time lifted his machete in the air and chopped off the head of the goat. Gene walked back and fell against the barbed wire fence, believing that Gabriel was going to hurt him.

"Come on, get up, don't be a coward, let's take the goat to the kitchen to remove the fur, cut it into pieces and have it ready for tomorrow," said Gabriel.

"Where are we going to cook it?" asked Gene.

"I've got a very good idea. Let's take it to Playita and make a good fricassee down by the beach," said Gabriel.

"That is a good idea," said Gene.

They invited two of my uncles. The following day the meeting place was at Bartolo's store. They bought all the ingredients needed for the fricassee, took all the utensils and moved towards Playita.

When they reached the place, Gene said, "There is something very important missing here."

"What is it?" the others asked.

"Without rum this is not going to taste the way it should," said Gene.

"Well then, let's go to La Llave and get a good gallon of rum from Colon's. They say he makes very good rum," said my uncle Rafael.

Both Gene and Rafael took off for La Llave. They had to walk up the rocky hills of Andino, go across the Perez mountain to reach the place. Rum was not ready. Colon told them to wait until the gallon filled up. They did that. After a few hours they took the rum and walked back to the beach. When they reached the place, "What the hell happened here? There is nobody around," they shouted.

They took a look around and found lots of bones spread around. Everything else had vanished.

"Oh my goodness! We have been made fools of," they kept shouting.

Later on I heard that the ones who were on the beach got so hungry that they couldn't wait any longer and they ate everything they had cooked.

Poor Gene, he was so anxious to have that fricassee and he didn't even smell it! He dreamed about eating it and eating under those beautiful palm trees and the fresh Caribbean breeze.

The Refrigerators

At this time of my life, Dominga bought a refrigerator. Now we didn't have to depend on the town's ice plant for cooling down beverages. Bartolo bought one for his store. These refrigerators had a kerosene burner to heat up the refrigerant. Electricity was not needed for operating them. They were very convenient for us. Now we didn't have to wait for Saturdays to have a cold Royal Crown or Coca-Cola. Now, Bartolo could sell cold beers every day. Dominga's ice box was a thing of the past. She then used the ice box as an extra cabinet to put things in the dining room.

Bartolo made delicious tropical fruit drinks. He used fresh coconuts, pineapples, guava and lemon.

The most sold soda drink was Royal Crown Cola followed by Coca-Cola. Nestor and I used to climb a Haguey tree after getting our Royal Crown and enjoyed that terrific taste sitting on the branches of the tree.

My First Movie

Luis, the younger son of Librada, came one day to invite me to watch a movie.

"Nello, have you ever seen a movie?" he asked me.

"What is that?" I asked.

"Well, it is something like a live picture that you watch. It moves as if it was real. Would you like to go with me?" he asked.

"Oh, yes, take me with you," I said.

He asked permission from my mother and we took off towards Monte Santo where he lived. Monte Santo was not too far from town. We walked to Monte Santo and late in the evening we walked to town. There we waited in the Plaza until they opened the gates to allow people in. I remember that the movie's title was *The Milkman*, enacted by some actor named Connors. We walked out after the movie. I was very happy to have watched my first movie and very grateful to my sister's brother-in-law. However, on our way back I was afraid of the Higueros area. It gave me the creeps. We had to pass by them on that dark night. After a short walk we were safely back in Librada's house.

Montanez's Circus and the Shipwreck

During that period of time, a man called Montanez came to Vieques with a whole bunch of chests, trunks, equipment and I don't know how many other things. He came in with his teenage daughter. He looked for a suitable place to install his circus. The place he liked most was located east of the Second Vocational Unit School. He charged ten cents per person to watch his shows. I watched few of his evening shows. He was the only actor and his daughter the only actress. He knew many tricks to entertain people. The one that impressed me the most was the hanging pole. He asked two strong men to go up on to the stage and tie a rope around his neck as tightly as they could. He asked them to hang him on a pole that he had placed on the stage. When the men were pulling him up by the neck, he moved his head sideways and fell down on the stage, totally unharmed.

His daughter was the clown, the actress, the dancer.

He created a character named the Dancing Mare. His daughter was placed inside some kind of doll resembling a mare and he guided her on their show.

His daughter was sick and tired of him because of his drunkenness. Most of the money he made he used for rum. He was drunk almost every day of the week. She didn't want to work no more and he constantly beat her and forced her to do the show every night. Tired of being abused, she decided to quit and go to some unknown place. She simply vanished. He looked for her all over the island, asking questions, spying on people to see if she was hiding somewhere, but never found her.

On a very dark night, while we were ready to sleep, we heard somebody screaming in the south.

Angel, my brother, heard the screams and said, "Let's go down to the Pass of the Boats! Somebody is drowning in there! Hurry, hurry everybody!"

The whole neighborhood of La Hueca got up and took off,

running down to the beach. When we reached the beach we saw a sailboat bouncing against the rocks, not too far in from where we were standing. My brother jumped into the sea, swam to the boat and there he found Montanez. He was dead drunk and could hardly stand up. My brother managed to get him out of the boat, swam back to the beach and laid him on the sands. There he laid, screaming and yelling for his daughter. My brother swam back to the boat and anchored it to one of the rocks. The following morning he would take care of it by looking for its owner. Luckily, the sails of the boat hadn't been hoisted up, otherwise he could have been carried deep into the sea by the tides and could have died of thirst and hunger.

After this incident Montanez disappeared and was never seen back in Vieques again.

Sara's Christmas Parties

Sara's Christmas party was the most looked forward to event of the year. The party was held at her house on Christmas Eve, year after year. Sara was Uncle Lolo's wife. All the women and men in the neighborhood used to get together days before the party to be assigned their respective duties. They sorted out the names of all participants for the surprise gifts, made the ornaments for the Christmas tree, cleaned the house, the furniture and made all sorts of preparations. Men bought some gallons of rum months ahead in order to cure them. My uncles Rafael and Cleo were in charge of roasting the pig. That was done on Uncle Rafael's lot, not too far east from our house. I loved that day because the wind carried the smell towards my house and made me feel hungry. My mother made the guava paste and jelly. The rest of the food was cooked at Sara's the same evening just before the party. They made a drink for women named the Bool. They mixed wine, beer, anisette, and added water, sugar and various cans of fruit cocktail in a very large bowl with plenty of ice. The ice was bought from the ice plant in town and preserved, wrapped up in sacks. This drink was made especially for women.

To the west of Uncle Lolo, on Andino's hills, grew a small conical thorny tree that was used as the Christmas tree. The name of the tree was Tintillo.

All the ornaments for the tree were made by Sara and her daughters. That evening, all the furniture was removed from the living and dining rooms to make the dancing area bigger. The living room furniture was placed outdoors and the dining room chairs and table were moved to the kitchen. There they placed all the goodies in some sort of order. The Christmas tree was placed in a corner of the living room and all the presents placed underneath as usual. The musicians had a space to the right of the tree. This position made it look very nice. Just before evening, all the participants and invited guests moved in. The musicians, as usual, were Tony Cigar and Manuel. The party started with music and dancing. In the beginning they played and danced rumbas, and all sorts of joyful music. As time passed by and the drinks were having an effect, the music started to slow down. The program included poems, imitations, joke telling, relating the humorous past events of the neighborhood and many other acts for entertaining. My mother was the perfect imitator. She had the ability to imitate the voice of any person. She spent a good part of the evening imitating because the people kept asking her for more and more. The Bool was served only to women and the cured rum to men. Music continued until the following morning. Food was served just before midnight and the presents were given away right after supper. All of us kids were kept out of the house, but we watched very closely. There was a Flamboyant tree in front of the house. I used to climb up that tree to watch all the program and all the funny things that happened during the party. Men and women were so drunk that they fell down and couldn't stand up on their own, others ran down to the bushes to throw up, others just watched and laughed at the ridiculous behavior of some. All night long there was happiness and joy. People loved that party. It was the only yearly party held in any house in the neighborhood and of many neighborhoods around. Never was there a serious incident or even a fight. Out of this party, many marriages came about. All the daughters of Uncle Lolo met their husbands-to-be at these parties, as well as many of the neighborhood girls.

My sister Alice told me that there was one curious thing at Uncle Lolo's. She said that there was a spring of a black oil coming from the ground. She said that it had a strong odor that she couldn't remove easily.

On Our Way

After the Christmas season was over, all the men and women had to return to their normal daily routine and the kids had to return to school. My brother Nestor had already graduated from twelfth grade and worked at the store of Juan in Monte Santo. Later he decided to move to San Juan. In San Juan he was hired by one of the newspapers to work in the arts department as a cartoonist and to retouch pictures. There he married a girl from Santurce. After he married, he was drafted into the U.S. Marine Corps due to the Korean conflict.

I was attending school in the Second Vocational Unit. At this time every home had a battery radio. The route to school was not too bothersome, because we could listen to music all the way from home to school. The favorite program in the morning was called *Your Happy Awakening*. This radio program had music, news and lots of humor.

The Road to La Esperanza

I was already a teenager and I started to go to La Esperanza on Saturdays. La Esperanza was the place for entertainment at weekends for people who couldn't go to town. There, they had juke boxes and we used to play music and dance with the girls of that place. The way to La Esperanza was due east until we reached the crossroads at Source. Right at the crossroads there was a small store belonging to Henry the Red. There he used to sell sausages, sauces, in general he sold all sorts of canned food. His most important product was rum. The veterans from the Second World War used to get together every Saturday in that place to drink, get drunk and fight. There was a fight now and a fight later on, as many fights as they could withstand until they got tired.

Close to the south of the small store lived Regino. He had a bar at La Esperanza. He had a black car that he parked looking down the slope on the road next to his house. It happened that one day my brother Angel and one of his drunkard friends took a chance and decided to go for a ride in the car. They went downhill until the car moved to the side of the road and hit a tree near a ridge. They left the car right there and took off to their homes. The next day the police came to arrest Angel and his friend Broda Ba. They were taken to the judge in town.

"Now let me see. You are accused of driving a car without permission and to have damaged that car," said the judge.

They stood silent, without even uttering a word.

"Who was driving the car?" asked the judge.

"Nobody," answered Broda Ba.

"What do you mean by nobody? How did that car move away?" asked the judge.

"Very simple, we pushed it downhill and jumped into it," said Angel.

"Who was in the driver's seat?" asked the judge.

"Nobody, we pushed the car downhill and both of us sat on

the rear seat," answered Broda Ba.

The judge put both hands on his forehead stood up and said, "For all the devils in this life, I can't believe you are alive!"

The judge's sentence for both was to share the cost of repair of the car, plus ten days' jail in the Spanish Fort. The judge talked to both of them after he had read the sentence. He scolded them for a while until Broda Ba interrupted him and said, "Hey, Joe, don't talk to me like that. You know that you make a living because there are scoundrels like me."

"Oh yeah, now you are going to be jailed for six more months for being disrespectful to this court of justice," said the judge.

On our way to La Esperanza, we passed by a small store atop a small hill. Downhill and to the right lived the Belardos. To the left there was a pathway where the Corcinos, the Romeros and the Guerras lived. There lived Juana Guerra, a neighborhood leader who tried many times to run as mayor of Vieques. She was a very strong woman and very helpful. She loved to help anybody however she could, especially those who needed the most help and those in distress.

Continuing the way to La Esperanza, we passed close to the beach and ahead we reached Regino's bar. That was our favorite place. He had two pretty daughters and a son. His daughters were available for dancing and entertaining people. They were not the only girls. Many girls from the neighborhood showed up to make that place the preferred dancing place.

Regino's place was located close to the pier. At the tip of that pier there was an old seawolf by the name of Hanie. He was a white man with white hair and beard. There, he spent day after day with his fishing rod. Nobody knew where he came from as he could speak five different languages. Many times he served as an interpreter for the foreigners who came through that seaport. His arms were always shaking from side to side. When somebody in Vieques had to shake for some reason, people said, "Oh boy, you are shaking just like Hanie at the tip of the pier."

At the back of Regino's place there was a small lagoon. The story goes that years ago two engineers came to make an analysis to determine how to empty the lagoon. While they were talking about it and taking some measures, there was a man sitting next to them, laughing. Since the lagoon was below sea level, they couldn't open a channel. So they figured out that they needed some mechanical equipment to do the job. In the meantime, the man besides them continued laughing. They didn't pay attention to the crazy man and left the place with some sort of a plan. The following day the engineers came back to take more measures and to continue their analyses.

"Hey, what is going on here! The lagoon is empty! How could that happen! There is no equipment on this island that could have done that in a single night!" they argued.

Not too far from them was the laughing man. The man laughed so much that he had to lay on the sands to continue laughing. After that incident the man was named the Loco Man of the Lagoon.

That incident became an unsolved mystery.

On the road to the north of La Esperanza town, there was a mansion built by Monsieur Mirat, a French farmer. The mansion had a wide balcony around it and a stable of horses down to the south of it. The story goes that this mansion was built by a gentleman who wanted to get married and bring his beloved wife over from France. He owned all the land surrounding his mansion. It was a very large farmland area. He married his beloved and brought her to Vieques. When she came in, she immediately missed the social life that she was used to in France. Sooner than expected she left him and returned to France. But before she left she said to her husband, "I am leaving because my father's horses are having a better life than I have in this remote place."

He left everything behind and followed her. All the land was seized by the Puerto Rico's Land Authority.

By this time the French language was almost disappearing as a daily spoken language in Vieques. You could no longer hear those morning greetings,

"*Bonjour, mon ami.*"

"*Comment vous portez-vous?*"

"*Comme ci, comme ça. Et vous?*"

"*Je vais très bien.*"

Then, they continued their conversation about their

plantations, harvesting and business.

For some time the Land Authority used this land to plant sugarcane and after the sugarcane industry came to an end, they planted pineapples. Pineapple plantations extended to the navy land west of La Hueca and covered all land belonging to the Land Authority. A pineapple processing and canning plant was installed at La Esperanza. That was a project to substitute the sugarcane. But private farm owners didn't trust the government plans and dedicated their land to pastures and cattle. The farmers were right. The pineapple industry was a total failure. All plantations were abandoned. The poor planning and the lack of professional expertise on the matter made it disappear quicker than anybody could ever imagine. One of the main reasons for its failure was that the harvested pineapples were too big and didn't fit in the processing machines.

They started another project. They planted on the same land a cereal named sorgo. This cereal grew on a plant that resembled the corn. It bore a grain that looked like black pepper and was almost the same size. This was another failure. I don't know what happened and why all the plantations were also abandoned. Ever since they abandoned these plantations we took advantage of the situation and fed the pigs with this cereal.

We tried to have some fun during our return from La Esperanza back to our homes. We always figured out a way to have some fun.

One of those evenings, my friend Lilo decided to serenade Catalina, the daughter of Pedro Ponce. He always carried his guitar everywhere he went on weekends. So, that evening coming back from La Esperanza, he invited me to sing in front of Catalina's room in the Pearl's neighborhood. We took a left from the main road into the pathway that led to her house. We started to play and sing and suddenly I heard a sound, as if something had fallen inside the house.

"Could that be the girl?" Lilo asked.

"I don't believe that. It sounded like something metallic that fell on the floor," I said.

Suddenly the front door opened and an old man with a huge machete ran towards us, yelling, "Get the hell out of here, there are no women in this house and you stupid kids don't let me sleep in peace."

We ran as fast as we could to avoid being hurt by that crazy old man. The guitar played like a waltz, with the air passing through the strings while we were running.

"Where did you take me to, Lilo?" I asked.

"I took you to Catalina's house," he answered.

"Are you nuts? We were at the house of a crazy madman," I said.

"She was there. The problem is that her father is very jealous of her and he doesn't want her to fall in love with anybody," Lilo said.

We went ahead until we reached Lolo's store. There, we sat on the stairway to rest for a while. While we were there, we heard people singing in Huerta's home to the north of us.

"Did you hear that?" asked Lilo.

"It sounds like one of those sung prayers that they do occasionally. Let's go and find out," I said.

We went across the road and walked north through a narrow pathway towards Huerta's house. When we reached the place, we saw all the people singing the rosary in the living room. At this moment Lilo farted.

"Ooph, Lilo, that was a stinky fart! What the hell did you eat?" I asked.

"Shut up and let's get the hell out of here," Lilo said and continued, "I ate four boiled chicken eggs with lots of red hot peppers."

I started walking in front of Lilo towards Lolo's store. We went across the road, and when we reached Lolo's store, Lilo passed close to Berto.

"Damn it, Lilo, you stink," said Berto.

When I got close to Lilo I noticed that the fart had followed us or that most of it was still remaining in his gabardine khaki pants. I told Lilo, "Go to back the road, walk back and forth and try to get rid of it by shaking your pants."

Lilo did as I told him and when he came back to the store we heard a scream on the road.

"My God, somebody left a fart hanging in the air!"

The scream came from Jesus Skerret. "I had to get off my horse in order to breathe fresh air."

At that instant a woman coming down the pathway from Huerta's house asked Skerret, "Did you mention a fart?"

"Yes, I crashed against a ball of stinky air when I was coming up the road and I had to get off my horse," he said.

"Well, I also had to get the hell out of Huerta's house for the same reason. We were singing the rosary when a mass of stinky air got inside the house and we almost died of asphyxia. Isn't that strange? Everybody in the house swore that no one farted," she said.

In the meantime, we were listening to their conversation with our mouths shut. We couldn't believe what we heard. Thank God, there was no air traffic in our area. Otherwise that thing moving up into the atmosphere could have caused an air disaster when smelled by an airplane pilot.

The Navy is Back

At the end of the decade of the forties, the threat of a war in Korea was imminent. Since this was the case, the navy returned to Vieques to occupy the abandoned territories. This time they were a better organized outfit. This time they didn't hire any civilian personnel to help rebuild the abandoned areas. They started to repair and rebuild the magazines, the fences and the roads. The U.S. Marine Corps with its engineering group took over all that work.

All our happiness came to an end. No trips to the western side were allowed. They placed a very powerful lamp on top of the hills of Andino to check for trespassers at night. From now on we couldn't hunt, fish, go for firewood or catch crabs in the lagoon mangroves. That was the very end of the good times and of our hope of getting back the life on the western side. The manner in which they returned gave us a hint that the land was unrecoverable. They came with a great number of war boats that were anchored on the south coastal waters of the island. That was a great spectacle for us kids. At night the lights in these many ships resembled a big city on the sea. We had never seen anything like it before. We spent many evenings at Bartolo's to watch the spectacular show. The boat that impressed me the most was the Hospital Boat. It one was a very big one, all painted white, with a very big red cross on each side of it. We could watch the aircraft carriers, destroyers, landing crafts and many others. The maneuvers started with many fighter planes, those fighters that had one propeller engine. They populated the sky by the hundreds. The maneuvers were held at the eastern end of the island. The paratrooper planes dropped hundreds of them that made the sky look dark during the day.

Thousands of marines had come to Vieques for training purposes. Many of them had their camps north of El Sapo. They were fed with C-rations during that period.

One day, during the afternoon a whole bunch of marines showed up in our neighborhood. They walked and looked around as if they needed something. Three of them approached my house. My sister got scared and hid in her room. One of them yelled, "I am hungry!"

I could understand English because all our textbooks in school were in English and I liked to learn as much as I could. Our way of pronouncing words was not the American way. It tended to be more on the British side. But I managed to learn the American accent.

My mother came to me and asked, "What is going on? What do they want?"

"They say that they are hungry," I told my mother.

One of them approached me and said, "Come on, little boy, if you understand some of my words, please tell your mama that we are looking for home-made food. We are tired of C-rations."

I told my mother exactly what they had said.

"Tell them that there are few baked arepas left in the kitchen, but not enough to fill their bellies," she said.

I explained to them what my mother had said.

"But can't she cook something for us? We will pay for whatever," they said.

At that instant my mother took a good look at those youngsters. She felt sorry for them and with a mother's heart totally open for them, she came to me and said, "Take them to the back of the house and tell them to kill two of the biggest chickens and bring them over. I'll fry them."

I took them to the backyard, they killed two of the biggest chickens with their bayonets and brought them over to my mother. She boiled a pot of water and put the chickens in it to remove the feathers and clean them up. Then she came to me and said, "Take these ten cents and go to Bartolo's store and buy two ice bars."

At that moment my sister came out of the room. She felt that those kids were decent. She didn't fear to be raped anymore. She could talk some English. They started a conversation with her, moved inside the house and laid on the living room floor. Meanwhile, my mother continued working in the kitchen, getting the food ready. The fried chicken smelled so good that the youngsters got up and went to the kitchen to continue smelling.

"Oh my goodness, I'm starving, I can't wait!" they yelled.

My sister took the two ice bars, put them in a jar of spring water from Andino's well and placed it on the dining table. My mother finished frying the chicken, placed the pieces in a basket with baked arepas and put them on the table. Their hunger was apparent. They jumped on the food like hungry beasts. My mother laughed and enjoyed watching them eat.

"I've never had such a great meal in my whole life. I think I will never forget this. Ask your mom how much we owe her," said one of them.

I told my mother about it and she said, "They are like my sons, I am not going to accept any money, they are paying me with their satisfaction, to see them happy is enough."

When they finished eating they laid back on the floor and continued talking to my sister.

One of them fell asleep and started to snore.

"Is there any place around where we could get some cold beers?" one of them asked Alice.

"Nello, show them the way to Bartolo's," Alice told me.

One of them slapped the face of the sleeper.

"Get up! You lazy bastard! Let's go get some cold beers."

I went down the pathway and showed them the way to Bartolo's store.

One day when I was in front of Bartolo's store, I saw the front wheel of a jeep come off and go downhill, off the road. The front end axle was broken and the jeep hit the barbed wire fence and stopped right there. I ran to see if the driver was hurt or if I could be of any help. The marine stepped out and asked me, "Do you understand English?"

"Yes," I said.

"Do me a favor, go to the camp down the road and tell one of my buddies to come and help me. Explain to them what happened here," he said.

I ran down the road to their camp, north of El Sapo. When I went across the fence one of them stopped me and took me by the arm.

"Hey, kid, people are not allowed into the camp. Go back to where you came from," he said.

"I came to tell you that one of your friends has had an accident up the road, not too far from here, and he needs help to repair his jeep," I said.

"I don't believe you. Get out!" he said.

"Hey, that kid must be telling the truth. I know that kid. He is the son of the woman who cooked for us a few days ago," said one of them.

"Okay, kid, tell me exactly what happened."

I explained the best I could. Two of them got some tools and spare parts and took off up the road. When we reached the place the marine was downhill, still looking for the loose tire. He found it and took it up. Meanwhile, the other marines were replacing parts of the jeep. After they finished repairing the jeep, the driver came to me and asked, "Where did you learn English?"

"At school. We study English every day," I said.

"I would like to meet your English teacher. Who is he?" he asked.

"He's not a he, she is a pretty girl," I said.

"A pretty girl? Tell her that one of these days I will meet her. Tell me, where is your school?" he asked.

I explained to him and gave all the details of the location of the school. After everything was all right they thanked me and left the place.

A few days had passed. I had told my English teacher about the accident and about the promised visit of my friend.

At exactly the time of my English class, the marine showed up. I saw his jeep coming uphill and parking in front of the room.

"There he is, Miss," I said.

"You are right, now I can see him," she said.

"Can I get up and look for him, Miss?" I asked.

"Yes, you may. Go get your friend and bring him into the classroom," she said.

The marine was a handsome youngster from the state of Oklahoma. My teacher, Gloria, was a pretty young girl who had won various beauty contests. She had a Bachelor of Arts from the University of Puerto Rico. When he came into the classroom something strange happened. They stood in front of each other, eye to eye, without even greeting one another.

My goodness, this is love at first sight! I thought.

The silence continued for a while until one of the kids said, "Please wake up!"

Everybody laughed and then they started to talk and continued talking for some time.

I never thought that I was going to be the witness of a marriage to be. After that conversation was over he said goodbye to us and left.

A few days later my teacher came up to me and said, "Do you know something?"

"No, I don't, tell me," I said.

"I am about to marry your friend, he is visiting me at home almost every day of the week."

They got married in a ceremony at her home. She gave me a wedding picture that showed her brother, Robinson, her husband and herself. Robinson was a civil engineer. She left for Oklahoma with her husband and about a month later she was back in Vieques. When I saw her, I asked, "Where is my friend?"

"He is in Oklahoma," she said.

"When is he coming back?" I asked.

"He is not coming. I left him."

"I can't believe that, you looked so much in love with each other that it makes it impossible to believe in that separation. What happened there?" I said.

"That place was hell, either too cold or too hot. He had a farm with lots of cattle on it and far from everywhere. He also wanted me to get up at four o'clock in the morning to milk the cows. That, I couldn't stand. I told him that I was not a farm girl and that I could never be. My hands were delicate and I was going to keep them that way forever. He was mad at me and tried to beat me. That was the end of the marriage," she explained to me.

I remember another case when a young marine fell in love with one of Gabriel's daughters. He was from Pennsylvania. Lygia Garambois was a blue-eyed pretty teenager. That marine was stationed at the camp north to El Sapo. Every afternoon he came down the road to Lygia's house and sat in there. Both watched each other without talking. She couldn't speak English and he couldn't speak Spanish. Communication was very difficult. He used some of us kids as interpreters for his messages to her. Since there was no progress he decided to quit the relationship.

After Gloria married, marriages with marines continued for some time. Many were successful, others weren't. Some remained living in Vieques forever and became successful businessmen.

The High School

After my graduation from the ninth grade, I worked for the pineapple plantations during the summer vacation period. That money was to be used for high school tuition fees, books and other needs. The books used in our high school were ordered from England.

This time we, the countryside kids, didn't have to look for room and board in town. The mayor of the island bought a station wagon to take us to school on a daily basis. This was free of charge. We waited for the car by the front gate of Dominga's farm. The students from La Hueca were the farthest from town, for this reason we had to take the first trip that was at five o'clock in the morning. We were taken to town that early and left in the Plaza close to the high school. There we waited until eight o'clock when classes started. The high school was a European-style building made with bricks and lumber.

Many times we used to go to the bakery up the main street to buy a loaf of bread with butter. There was an elementary school named San Francisco in front of the bakery. We used to sit there, on the sidewalk in front of the school, and share and eat our bread.

Walking up San Francisco street, was when I first met and fell in love with my golden girl Magaly Simmons.

Gran Diablo's Chase

On one of those mornings, while we were cutting our bread to share it, Gilbert started to whistle a melody. Behind his back he heard somebody saying, "Stop right there, I've got you!"

When Gilbert looked back he saw Gran Diablo with a machete in his hand ready to chop him off. Gran Diablo was a madman in town. He was always barefoot, with his pants rolled up, and he carried a sack and a machete under his left arm. He didn't like to be whistled at. Kids made fun of him by whistling and hiding. They enjoyed watching the madman getting angry.

When Gilbert saw the angry madman behind him, he immediately ran down the street. Gran Diablo ran after him with his arm high up holding the machete, ready to swing it down on Gilbert's head and yelling, "Stop right there. You scoundrel! I've got you!"

And the chase continued on and on until they disappeared from our sight. We went down the street back to the Plaza. We saw Gran Diablo with his machete raised up, chasing Gilbert across the Union Street and yelling, "Stop, stop, stop! You scoundrel!"

We continued walking down the main street and, across the Duteil Street, there they went.

"Stop right there. I've got you!"

We sat in the Plaza to wait for the outcome of this problem. On that silent morning the only sound close or far away from us was, "Stop, stop! You scoundrel!"

Later on we saw Gilbert totally exhausted, walking towards the Plaza.

"Oh my goodness! What a run so early in the morning!" said Gilbert.

"Why didn't you stop? He has never harmed anybody. He is just a nervous person," one of the students told Gilbert.

"Do you think that I am going to stop at a madman with a

machete in the air, ready to chop my head off? Don't forget that there is always a first time for everything."

At that instant Gran Diablo came to the Plaza. He was exhausted also. Gilbert stood up in a hurry, getting ready to flee away from him again.

"Look, boy, next time I'll get you," Gran Diablo said and he walked away.

"Oh, how I wish to get out of this devilish town!" said Gilbert.

The Fiestas

The yearly fiestas in town were held late in the month of July. We liked to stay on Fridays after school in order to enjoy part of them. A group of countryside students missed the bus on purpose, so as to stay on until late at night during the fiestas. We liked to enjoy all of those things that we could see only once a year, like amusement machines and those candy stores. The fiestas started on a weekend, lasted throughout the week and closed down the following weekend. We sat in the Plaza until evening, waiting for all the activities to start. For some refreshments, I liked to go to the soda fountain named The Green Room. Side by side, there was the soda bottling factory of Don Felipe Serrano. It was located on the widest street in town. The street was made wide enough by the early French settlers to be the town's boulevard. Most of the activities of the fiestas, like horse racing, parades and other shows, were held on that wide street, but the Plaza was my favorite attraction. There was dance music played every night, and we could dance in the open and have all the fun in the world. The girls were a favorite attraction also. They dressed in many colors and used to wink at us, walk by, look back and laugh at us. We walked around the Plaza by following an order. The girls walked counterclockwise and the boys clockwise. That way we could meet many times at night and talk a little to each other while walking around. The girls, who were wearing different fashions of many colors, gave a beautiful colored look to the Plaza. They wore their skirts to the knees and their blouses had short sleeves due to the hot tropical weather.

Most of the official dances were held at the Ocean View Night Club. This Club was located by a ridge at the northern side of town, on the street to the piers. It was a very comfortable place for this type of activity. I could never forget Bueyon, the waiter. He was after every youngster, watching our behavior.

After all activities were over that night, all youngsters got together and started on the way back home. We had to walk about five to six miles but it was worth it. It was a nice walk. Not too nice on very dark, cloudy or rainy nights, but very pleasant on moonlit nights. We reached our houses to take a bath and remove all the sweat from our bodies to feel refreshed and go to sleep. In bed we would go over and think about all the interesting things that had happened that night. The next day, on Saturday afternoons, we used to get together at the crossroads of La Esperanza, by Henry the Red's store.

"Do you remember that horse that slid and fell down in front of the Plaza?"

"How about how frightened we got when that bull showed up in the middle of the road last night?"

"Did you ask for the name of that girl that you met in the Plaza?"

"Do you know her parents?"

And conversation went on and on until dark.

Guateen's Run

Guateen had a girlfriend whom he had met at the fiestas. On weeknights he could go to town on Don Diaz's black horse and enjoy more of the fiestas. He used to date his girl on Friday evenings after school, at Monte Santo's chapel. He had a friend who had a girl whom he also met at the chapel. He lived in the neighborhood of El Pilon. They agreed that after the prayers they would take the girls home, say goodnight and meet back at the chapel. From there they would walk back home at night.

One night, for some reason, Guateen waited at the stairway of the chapel but El Cano didn't show up. Tired of waiting, he took off alone down the road to La Hueca. Like many Fridays after school I used to stay at Don Diaz's to help him out on the farm on Saturday mornings. All of a sudden, I heard a noise at the stairway of the house. It was around nine thirty. I got up, opened the door and I saw Guateen lying on the floor, all exhausted. His shirt was all torn and his arms were bleeding.

"What the heck happened to you?" I asked.

"I am frightened, you can't imagine how scared I am. I ran so fast that you would never believe it," he said.

"It is only nine thirty. Where were you?" I asked.

"I was at Monte Santo with my girl, Cano didn't wait for me," he said.

"Did you take a ride? You couldn't have made it that fast from Monte Santo to this place," I said.

"I told you that I ran as fast as I could," he said.

"I still don't believe you. Go to bed and we will talk tomorrow," I said.

"Look, let me explain this to you. When I was walking up the hill of Martineau, I heard steps behind me. I stopped and the steps stopped also. I looked around and didn't see a thing. I started to walk slowly and the steps followed me as slowly as I walked. Then I walked faster and the steps were faster too. I stopped again and took a good look around. At that moment I remembered the legend of the ghosts who, flying on top of furs, appeared in that area. It gave me the creeps. Quickly, I started to run as though fleeing from the devil. That is why I made it back so fast," he said.

"I still don't believe you," I said and went to bed.

The next day, on Saturday afternoon as customary, we took off to the crossroads of La Esperanza at Source. There Guateen started to talk about his previous night's adventure but nobody believed his story.

"No human being can run that fast," they said.

"Get off my back, and tell that lie to the horses," others said.

"But ask Nello, my brother. He can tell you the truth," he kept insisting.

At that instant we saw Cano coming down the road of Source.

"How come you didn't wait for me last night, Guateen?" he asked.

"Where were you? You can't imagine how scared I got last night with some steps I heard behind me," said Guateen.

"Don't tell me that. You don't know what happened to me and how scared I got last night. When I was coming down the Mine hill's road something passed by my side so fast that it looked like a spirit fleeing away from hell. It looked like a boy. But it couldn't have been a boy because it was not touching the ground. I couldn't figure out what the hell it was. I got so scared that it gave me the shivers," Cano said.

Before Cano continued everybody burst into laughter. Now they believed Guateen's story.

Le Guillou (Mambiche)

My brother Nestor had already completed his training at Parris Island and was stationed on Cam Le Jeune, North Carolina. He already knew that his amphibious landing exercise was going to take place in Vieques. He rented a house in the Le Guillou neighborhood. This neighborhood was a suburb of town, to the south of it. There was a yellow bridge to get to the neighborhood from the main road. It was an ancient bridge built with bricks over the path of the Le Guillou brook. I noticed that the middle column that held that bridge had a triangular shape. This shape prevented the flow of water from pushing the column. It cut the water flow into half, thus nullifying the force of the water.

My mother was having problems with my older brother, Angel. He had become a drunkard. His alcoholism was so severe that he had become very aggressive. That was an unbearable situation for my mother. She explained the situation to Nestor and he asked her to move with his wife to Le Guillou. She sold the animals to Uncle Cleo because in the new house animals were prohibited. The lot was too small.

That was another step in our route to destiny. We knew that the end was far away, this was not our house, and that in the near future we would have to move again.

My mother continued to do laundering for various families and for some marines who needed this service. I used to leave high school at two o'clock in the afternoon after my English class. I got a job at the store of Berto Diaz in town for six dollars a week for a seven-day week. That income would help in our needs.

Our house was close to Miss Gittings', my former first grade teacher.

One day I heard Miss Gittings yelling at somebody in the street. I looked out and there, on the sidewalk in front of her house, laid her father, dead drunk.

"Get up you, drunkard!" she yelled in English.

"I no speek eenglees, me speek paneesh, no understand!" he yelled back to her.

"I tell you again, get up and get inside!" she yelled again.

"I no speek eenglees, me speek paneesh, no understand!" he yelled back to her again.

They continued yelling at each other until Miss Gittings gave up, took him by an arm and dragged him inside the balcony.

In front of us there lived a man who always dressed in the military way. He wore a very well-pressed military uniform and a red beret. He used to collect anything he could find in the street. He used to take all the garbage and toss it into his backyard. He kept the street clean from leaves, loose papers and whatever was dropped there. His relatives used to come periodically to clean his backyard to avoid the accumulation. He was not in his senses. Every time anybody talked to him, he said, "Look into the books, everything is written. Read the books and you will find out."

My brother Nestor, periodically, came back from Camp Le Jeune to Vieques. He told me that there was something he couldn't understand. All the marines received an overseas pay while in the Caribbean, but that compensation was denied to the Puerto Rican-born marines.

The Korean War was on. The Selective Service System was sending all qualified youngsters to Fort Buchanan for physical examinations. This with the intention of recruiting as many youngsters as possible to be sent to Korea. Just days before our high school graduation, a large group of students were sent to Fort Buchanan. We almost missed the graduation ceremony. Fortunately, we made it back on time.

A tragic incident happened then. One of our schoolmates by the name of Juan Campos went out to take care of his father's cattle. While he was walking he inadvertently kicked a live shell left by the marines. This shell exploded and killed Juan. We missed Juan during our graduation ceremony and for some time. After our summer vacation most of us were drafted into the U.S. army. We were sent to Camp Tortuguero to be trained as light weapons infantrymen. We spent six months of hard training in all defense and offense military tactics. After being trained, our group was sent to Japan on a military ship via the Panama Canal. There, we spent a few weeks at the seaport of Sasebo on Kyushu Island before being assigned to the permanent outfit in Korea. I was moved to Korea on a destroyer and landed in Inchon, Korea. From there some of us took a train to our destination on the occupied side of North Korea where the Third Infantry Division was stationed. There I was assigned to the Sixty-fifth Infantry Regiment. After the ceasefire period and after the declaration of the end of the war, the Third Infantry Division colors were moved back to the United States. At this time I was assigned to the Twenty-first Infantry Regiment of the Twenty-fourth Infantry Division.

During this time my brother Nestor was already out of the Marine Corps and went to the University of Puerto Rico. He started to study agricultural sciences. My mother went back to our former house in La Hueca as she didn't want to pay any more rent. But the ghost of drunkenness of our older brother was still there. She decided to buy a house at Le Guillou with the money we had saved to flee away again from her alcoholic son. When Angel found out about this, he sold the house and moved to the U.S. Virgin Islands.

After my assignment in Korea was over, I returned to Vieques. There, my brother Nestor convinced me to go to the University of Puerto Rico to get an engineering degree. Taking advantage of the GI Bill, I decided to do so as the money assigned for tuition and expenses was appropriate.

The Cannon, Doctor Karl and the Grapefruit Bitch

The Cannon neighborhood was located west of town, by the cemetery. That neighborhood was famous for the prostitution business that flourished there. They had their bars and the rooms and whatsoever to please the men who wanted some fun and sex. Ever since I was a kid, I had known about this place. I have heard many stories about this place from the youngsters and men who have been there. That place spelt bad news in Vieques. Many fights and crimes took place there. Women liked to cut the face of another woman for revenge or jealousy.

During that time the government of Puerto Rico established a health program to check every prostitute in town. Steeped in extreme poverty due to the loss and lack of jobs, prostitution became an important source of income. Many marines had to go to the Cannon neighborhood to satisfy their sexual urges.

The Puerto Rican government hired an American doctor to take care of the Health Department in Vieques. He was known as Doctor Karl. Examining all the prostitutes was his priority. The government had to prevent the spread of any venereal disease. The Health Unit issued a health card to all the prostitutes to identify them and to make sure that they were already checked and healthy.

Doctor Karl hired someone to help his wife with the housekeeping duties. Since the prevention of venereal diseases was so important, Doctor Karl moved through the island to look for information on non-declared prostitutes. He wanted people to tell him about any suspicious girl. He made a list of all the girls whom people suspected or knew that they had something to do with prostitution. He then issued appointments to those girls to be checked in a private way. He checked everyone on the list but one. That one was named the Grapefruit Bitch. He looked all over the island and couldn't find her. He even spied on people secretively to see if someone was hiding her.

"Hey you, do you know where to find the Grapefruit Bitch?" he asked.

"Look, Doctor, I've got no grapefruit in my backyard, and no bitches in my house," some answered, making fun of the situation.

"Hey you, I am looking for the Grapefruit Bitch, and I can't find her. Can you tell me where she lives?" he continued asking.

He even moved inside houses and said, "Tell the Grapefruit Bitch to get out of that room."

Many people didn't know anything about a prostitute named Grapefruit.

"The people don't want to give me information, but I am going to find her, even if I have to go to the moon," he said to himself.

He remembered the man who had given him the information about that girl. He went to his house and said, "You are going to tell me where to find the Grapefruit Bitch."

"I really can't tell you exactly because she only shows up at night for a while and then disappears," the man said.

"Okay, let's go to my house and you describe her. I'll take notes of your description on a piece of paper. You have to be specific about how she looks and where you have met her. This way I'll find her in no time," he said.

They went to Doctor Karl's home. They sat down in the living room and Doctor Karl said, "Wait for me. I'll be back in a moment with a pencil and paper. But first let's have a cup of coffee. Hey girl, bring us a cup of coffee as soon as you can!" he yelled at the girl in the kitchen.

When the girl came into the living room the man became so pale that it was immediately noticed by Doctor Karl.

"What the hell is wrong with you? You look so pale. There is no blood on your face! Did you fall in love with that girl?" Doctor Karl asked.

The man was so surprised that he couldn't even talk. He was practically paralyzed.

"Shhhhe is, shhhhe is the girl you are looking for..." the man said.

"Whaaaaat! Don't tell me that she is the Grapefruit Bitch! I can't believe this!"

He put both hands at the back of his head and yelled again, "I can't believe the Grapefruit Bitch is in my home. I've been looking all over the island, up the hills, down the hills and in every home, and the Grapefruit Bitch was living in my house!"

That was the gossip of the day that lasted for years in Vieques.

A Pause on the Course of the Route

Here, at this point in time I left Vieques to go to university. I make a pause on the course of the route. Many things happened before and after the continuation on our route to destiny, but that is another story.

Later on, more stories will be told about the remainder of the island's places and the ancient French, Portuguese, Spanish, other Europeans, Americans and British Isles' families who settled in Vieques forever.

Glossary

Algarrobo	A dusty-like pulpy fruit
Apreen	A Spiny tree that bears a fruit that looks like an olive but tastes like an apple
Arepa	Dough, shaped round like a bagel, either fried or baked
Beelee	A drink made with the pulp of the quenepa fruit mixed with rum or with water and sugar
Beeyard	A very popular children's game
Bruja	Dead or unemployment period
Cachasa	Carbonized peel of sugarcane produced by the sugar mill
El Sapo	The frog
Garapeen	Wire shaped like a hook to guide a wheel
Haguey	A tree with thick foliage, usually known as laurel from India
Higuera	An indigenous tree that bears a big spherical fruit with a very hard peel. This fruit is used to keep liquids. The pulp inside is removed leaving an orifice on top.
Jumaso	A rustic cigar
La Central	The sugar mill
La Hueca	The hollow
La Palma	The palm tree
Mascabado	Brown sugar in bars, not granulated
Playa Grande	Big beach
Playa Vieja	Old beach

Playita	Little beach
Pocito	Little well
Punta Arenas	Sandy point
Quenepa	A pulpy fruit with a hard peel
Saramba	A very big home-made top
Town	Isabel Segunda, the capital of the island of Vieques
Zafra	Sugarcane harvest period

Some of the earliest families that settled in Vieques for its colonization.

French	Le Grand, Le Brun, Vergè, La Vergne, Boulognèz, Delerue, Emerie, Garambois, Danois, Valois, Mireau, Du Bois, Maysonet, Monet, Monell, Brignoni, Velez, Choisne, Jean Pierre, Gastineau, Landreau, Durieux, Rucci and others.
Portuguese	Silva, Moreira, Portela, Pereira.
Irish	Mc Clat, O'Neill, Mc Faline.
British	Simmons, Shaw, Adams, Sanes.
British Isles	Hoggings, Galloway, Guishard, Williams, Gittings, Peterson, Richardson, Humphreys, Christian.
Spanish	Diaz, Morales, Lopez, Benitez, Rivera, Bermudez, Rodriguez, Castaño, Abreu, Velez, Belardo, Gonzalez, Sanchez, Pimentel, Ventura, Peña, Segui, Colon, Maldonado, Cruz, Navarro, Rios.

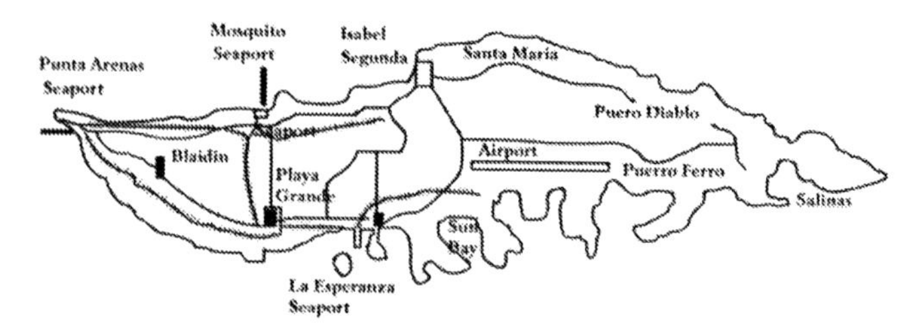

VIEQUES BEFORE 1940

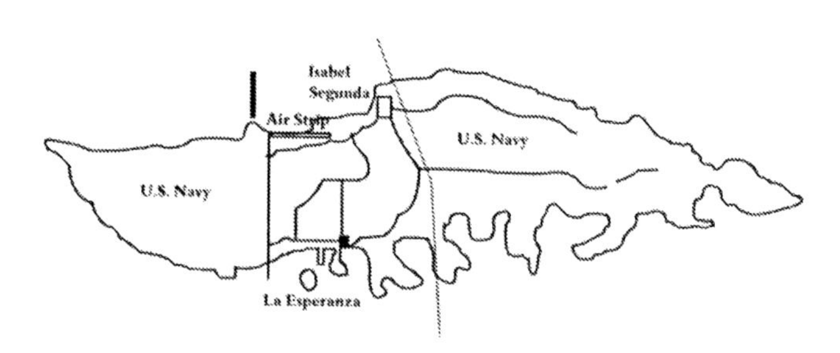

VIEQUES AFTER 1940

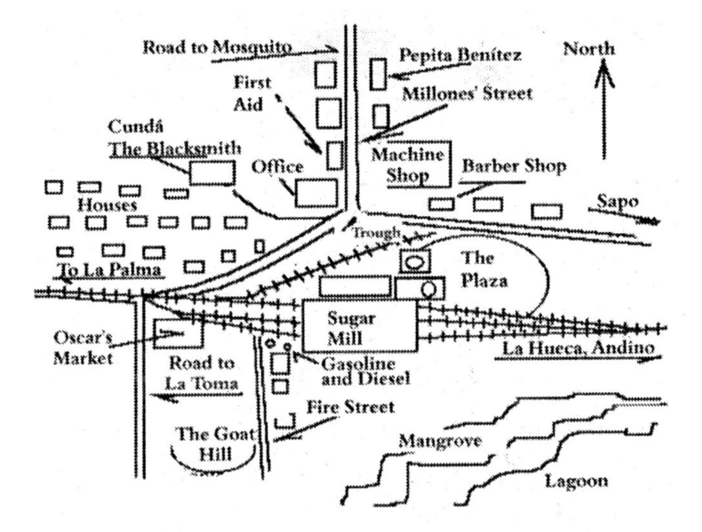

Playa Grande
(Before 1940)

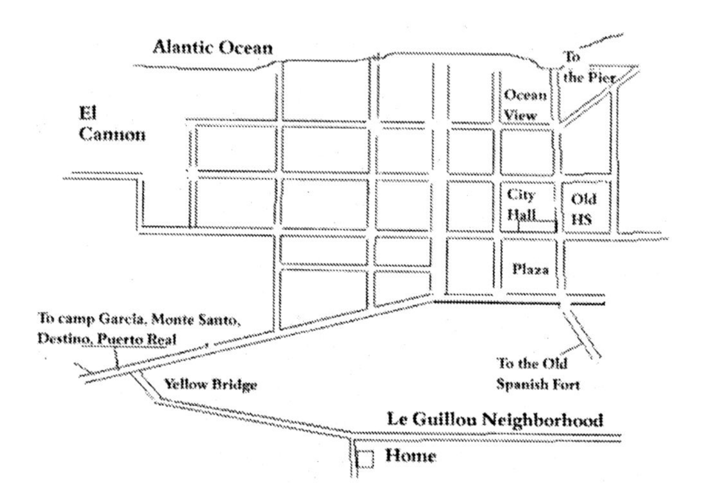
Alantic Ocean
El
Cannon
To
the Pier
Ocean
View
City
Hall
Old
HS
Plaza
To camp Garcia, Monte Santo,
Destino, Puerto Real
Yellow Bridge
To the Old
Spanish Fort
Le Guillou Neighborhood
Home

Isabel II

Printed in the United States
31226LVS00003B/3